ALL THEY WANT FOR CHRISTMAS

ANDIE J. CHRISTOPHER

Copyright © 2018 by Andie J. Christopher

All rights reserved.

No part of this book may be reproduced in any form or by any electronic or mechanical means, including information storage and retrieval systems, without written permission from the author, except for the use of brief quotations in a book review.

1

———

'T was the night before the night before Christmas, and there were only two couples left in the restaurant. Francesca Riley—half of one of the erstwhile pairs—had polished off her dessert, a truly transcendent chocolate torte smothered in delicate, smoky salted caramel.

She'd barely tasted it at all. All of her senses were honed towards the man sitting across from her—the tall, square-jawed New Englander currently picking at his food and moaning with pleasure at the flavor of his pear tart.

Frankie picked through the remnants of her dessert, finally putting her fork down with as much care as she could possibly summon. She'd been expecting a sparkling, diamond surprise from the moment they walked into the restaurant. Bouncing in her chair from the instant they were seated. She'd held up each glass of each wine pairing up to the light so as not to accidentally swallow a solitaire.

And…nothing.

Ted had been hinting at a proposal for the better part of six months. Every time someone mentioned a wedding, an engagement ring, a baby in her presence, she felt a pang in her chest about the status of her relationship—the relationship that she'd been hoping would change tonight.

For Christ's sake, she'd started dating him because the handsome politician had told the newspaper that he was looking for a wife. And she wanted to be a wife. Sure, he wasn't ideal. He didn't pay attention to what she was saying half the time, and he'd corrected her manners three times when they'd started dating. But he was six-four, had the aforementioned square jaw, and he knew how to find her clitoris without a flashlight.

That should be enough. It had to be enough.

She wasn't going to get the guy she really wanted. He'd made it clear that he wasn't the marrying kind and had the audacity to suggest that she wasn't either.

Well, she'd show him. With glossy engagement photos spread all over social media and an announcement in the *New York Times*. She had fantasies of Cary seeing the pictures and a single tear rolling down his face. She had other fantasies about him, but those were inappropriate to be having when she was sitting across from Ted—her soon-to-be fiancé.

So, she shook them out of her head, which finally caught Ted's attention.

"Is everything okay?" he asked.

Frankie smiled tightly. "Yes." Dammit, her voice sounded as high and thready as her nerves felt. She hated feeling like this. All she wanted was a sparkly ring on her finger when they got on the plane tomorrow to meet her family and celebrate the holidays. She could see the smile on her grandmother's face when they announced the news. No more admonishments about her being a "career girl" said in a tone like she was a "serial killer" instead of the vice president of a public relations firm that worked against climate change.

"Something's wrong." One of Ted's brows went up, and Frankie stifled a sigh. "You can tell me." He reached across the table and took her hand. She had to deliberately unclench it to string her sweaty fingers through his dry ones.

"I just—I thought that tonight was going to be a special night." This, dark shame slicked over her skin at the fact that she was *asking* him about this. After finding his "secret" Tinder profile a week ago, she'd almost called things off. And the titty pics he'd thought he'd kept angled away when he was texting someone the month before that had made her grind her molars. The shame was more about what she was prepared to accept—at least temporarily—to keep a man long enough that her grandmother wouldn't die thinking that she wasn't good enough.

Sure, he was handsome and marginally talented as a politician, but his average intelligence and obsession with his hair grated on her.

Again, she compared him unfavorably with Cary— whose tousled ginger locks always looked perfect, but who put no effort into them. No, when she was with Cary, all of his attention had been laser focused on her. Whatever they'd done together—in bed or out—had been all about her delight.

She shook her head again, twice as hard, trying to remember why she couldn't have that. She had to be married before her grandmother slipped into dementia because she didn't want the woman who had helped raise her to die without knowing that Frankie had made the life she wanted—even if being married to Ted was only kind of the life her grandmother wanted for her.

"Tonight is super special," Ted replied. "This dessert is *amazing*."

Frankie's nerves snapped, and she growled at him. He sat back in his chair, eyes wide. But she was not about to back down after she'd put nine months into this relationship. "Where is this going Ted?"

"To Minneapolis to meet your family?" He sounded truly bewildered. Well, wasn't that *special*?

"Where's my fucking engagement ring?" She would swear later that she hadn't meant to yell at him. It was just that she needed this to happen tonight. She didn't know if she would have another chance to show her grandmother that she wasn't a complete failure in her personal life.

Ted's face arranged itself into a mask off disgust and humor. He thought this was *funny*? "Listen, Frankie—"

Oh shit. She knew what came after this. The word "listen" was a bad sign. Fuck-ups at work always came after that word. Break-ups always came after that word. Bad news from a doctor always came after that word.

"I've been meaning to talk to you about where this is going."

Fuck. It was definitely not going in the right direction—up an aisle toward a priest at St. Anthony of Padua Church. "And where is this going?"

"I don't think it's a good idea for me to come home to Minneapolis with you." This motherfucker was going to feed her the most expensive tasting menu in D.C. before breaking up with her and sending her home for Christmas with an empty ring finger.

Goddammit. She could feel her grandmother's disapproval settle into her bones right then. She would slip away thinking that Frankie couldn't find a single man out of billions to settle down with. None of her professional success mattered, not to a woman from her generation.

There'd been times during college where her grandmother wouldn't even look at her if she didn't have a boyfriend. The rest of the family laughed it off as a quirk, but it felt like a weapon to Frankie.

"Could you just pretend for my grandmother?" She just laid out all her pride on the table, right then. She had no use for it anymore. "She's dying."

Ted bit his lip. He really thought that dumping her was funny. It was probably the right decision to break up with her, because she was going to kill Ted if she had to look at him for too much longer. "Frankie, I just think we want different things."

"But you said you wanted a wife!" Definitely yelling in the almost empty restaurant because several of the servers and the bartender looked up from their side work.

That's when she noticed that she and Ted were not the last couple—er, diners—in the restaurant. Something in her brain must have skipped over the tall, handsome red-haired man in the corner. Because if she'd seen him, she wouldn't have been worried about getting engaged that night. She would have been the one who broke up with Ted if she'd seen him next to Cary George—her favorite mistake.

Even though she'd just humiliated herself by demanding a proposal from a guy who was clearly dumping her, she watched the way Cary's elegant fingers adjusted his black-rimmed glasses, the way the veins in his forearms flexed with the motion, the quirk of his mouth that told her that he'd been watching the whole interchange.

And then the man across from him turned and grimaced at her. His dark hair and blue eyes tore a hole in her decorum even bigger than the one she'd ripped a few moments ago. It was as though he just threw off so much testosterone that *she* wanted to fight and brawl and fuck and never see Ted ever again. The man sitting across from the table was looking at her as though she was dessert, and it bolstered her flagging courage.

"C'mon *Ted*." She didn't question it. Humiliating herself in front of the only man she'd ever *wanted* to marry was bad enough. "You know that I'm the best you were ever going to do. And you got scared." She looked him up and down.

"That's not—"

She held up her hand. "No, you're just as chicken-shit as your opponent said you were." Her company had been hired to support Ted's campaign for Congress when they'd met. She'd made sure he won by getting to take actual stances on actual issues that people cared about instead of offering mealy-mouthed platitudes. She'd cleaned him up and made sure he won his campaign. Somehow in the process, she'd thought she'd molded him into an ideal fiancé that she could ride all the way to her grandmother's good graces.

But, to her shock, seeing Cary and his dinner companion here tonight, being reminded of how viscerally alive that she felt around her ex-lover, made her realize that she didn't need to make this mistake.

She could head home tomorrow and make up a constituent emergency, ply her grandmother with some bullshit about how Ted wanted to ask her permission before proposing, and then let the hateful old bat die knowing that she wouldn't be alone.

Because losing Ted wasn't a thing that would make her feel alone. Staying with him would.

"Get the check before you go, Ted."

"But you have to let me explain, Frankie—"

She reached over the table and put her hand over his mouth. God, she'd wanted to do that on a nearly daily basis since she'd started dating him. She'd never met a man who loved his own voice that much—and she'd worked on Capitol Hill after college.

"No, I don't." He tried to say something, but she gave him a look. She could feel Cary's amusement from across the room. He'd regularly irked her just to see her get angry and then fucked the anger right out of her. It was a game—a game she'd rather liked and would perhaps see about playing again when she returned after the holiday. He might not be marriage material, but she deserved a proper rebound after a hard election cycle and a motherfucker dumping her right after she'd cleaned him up into something respectable. "You're going to break up with me, because you realize that I'm better than you."

Ted furrowed his brow, and she laughed in his face. "Pay the check before you leave, Ted."

She let go of his face, stood, and took the glass holding the dregs of her wine.

Then—because it was Cary and she couldn't not—she walked over to their table and said, "Fancy meeting you here."

FRANCESCA RILEY HAD ALWAYS left Cary a bit gobsmacked. More force of nature than woman, at times he'd been unsure what to do with her. But there'd been something different about her tonight. He hadn't even noticed her until the yelling had started. And then, as soon as they'd locked eyes across the dining room, something had shifted inside her. He'd seen it.

Right now, he was back to gobsmacked. And that feeling with a person—any person—was not a comfortable thing for him. For example, the man sitting across from him was a known quantity. They'd been best friends at university and in—regular contact—in the years since.

Lucas Moore could not be more opposite to Francesca. Where she threw all of this feral energy out into the atmosphere, he tried to fade into the background. Job requirement and all that.

Cary honestly didn't know how they'd stayed friends given the disparity in their personalities. He and Francesca were far more alike, which was probably why their brief relationship had burnt out—in addition to his own reasons. But they were both extroverted and a bit a wild—nothing like Lucas' cold control that only cracked under very limited circumstances.

But Cary trusted Lucas with his life. The only thing he trusted Frankie with was to throw his life into chaos.

"Enjoy the after-dinner show?" The smile that didn't reach her eyes told him that she wasn't completely okay with the display she'd just bestowed upon them.

"I always enjoy your shows." He knew his words held double meaning. Knew that she was remembering how he used to sit in the arm chair next to his bed, roll up his sleeves, and order to strip off her slinky little cocktail dresses. Her hazel eyes went from the green of anger to the doe-brown of lust in that instant. Needing more of her, even though he was here with Lucas and had every intention of fucking him later, he motioned to a chair. "Please sit down."

Ever contrary, she stayed standing and offered her hand to Lucas, "Frankie Riley."

When Lucas cupped her delicate hand in his meaty paw, he swore he could see the snap of energy lighting up between them. And, even though they'd both been his lovers, jealousy wasn't even a miniscule part of his reaction. Rather, it turned him on beyond measure to see Lucas' body tense up and Frankie's spine lose most of its starch. Even more to see Lucas keep her hand as she slipped into the chair he'd pulled up. He liked seeing his friend touch her, and he wanted to touch both of them.

"What was all that about?" Lucas asked, his words clipped. Cary knew that he was thinking of ten ways to kill the man who had just hastily paid their check and vacated the restaurant. But only if he was still a danger to Francesca. Interesting that he'd taken such a liking to the woman so quickly. Knowing him for a decade and a half meant knowing that Lucas did not cotton to anyone at first sight. Bloody hell, it had taken him months to get the other man to smile. And that had taken a blow job.

"I came here thinking Ted was going to propose." Cary knew how much Francesca had wanted to be married and felt a pang that he didn't know how to be a husband. "And Ted didn't want a girlfriend anymore."

Lucas leaned forward and offered Francesca one of his rare smiles. "Ted is an idiot."

"He's of average intelligence," she replied. "I have the reports."

Cary reinserted himself into the conversation. "You did a great job with his campaign." During the few moments that he'd watched their interchange, he'd realized that her dinner companion had been one of her clients. And it had irked him that they'd apparently become something more.

Yet another reason he'd broken things off from her. He didn't like feeling jealous of anyone. It wasn't in his nature, and the fact that Francesca brought out such brutal envy in him did not sit well.

"Of course, I did." She broke her gaze away from Lucas—he understood the struggle—and looked at him, fire in her eyes. "I always do a fantastic job."

He found himself surprised that she was throwing out sexual innuendo. And then he had an idea. A dangerous idea. A sexy idea.

Lucas looked at him, grim set of lips returned when he grocked what Cary was thinking. Before his old friend could object, he motioned for the server. "We're going to need another bottle of wine."

2

———

Lucas knew what Cary was doing, and he wasn't entirely opposed. But he didn't know enough about the lovely Francesca to be totally on board. She was deeply disarming, to be sure, but inviting her to join them for their annual Christmas fuckfest—much more satisfying than sharing a pudding with his alcoholic father—well, he wasn't sure.

But he was curious, and that was enough for Cary to run with. He'd always barreled in and taken over, moving the people in his life like chess pieces in ways that pleased him. More often than not, Lucas was more than happy to go along. Though he was technically a spy—at least until he and Cary got their consulting firm set up—the greatest adventures in his life had been with his best friend and sometimes lover. That's how he knew immediately—from the moment Cary's eyes had lit with mischief staring at the couple across the restaurant—that this weekend was not going to go as planned.

Instead of indulging in the on-off affair that would switch to permanent off once they were officially in business together over the holiday, they would be doing the other thing that they'd been doing intermittently for years—sharing the delicious Francesca.

It would probably keep him from admitting to Cary that he was in love with him and had been hoping that this holiday wouldn't be the end of their affair. He wouldn't reveal the hope that they could somehow turn this into something permanent.

Instead, he would grumble to Cary privately, but he was a sucker for the other man. And fucking Francesca wouldn't exactly be hardship. He and his old friend had never had a possessive relationship like that. They'd just discovered that neither of them were precisely heterosexual when one of Cary's many girlfriends had wanted them both for a night. Cary—being Cary—had made sure the lady had gotten what she wanted. And he'd made sure that Lucas had gotten what he wanted as well—then and on every occasion they were in the same city since.

Whenever he came together with Cary, he felt as though he was coming home. More than going back to Manchester to visit his parents and sister. And definitely more than his sterile flat in London. Cary was his home, and he would give up the sex with him to keep that home someplace he could be all the time. But he didn't have to like it.

But now that they were going into business together, Cary had a strict policy of not mixing business with pleasure. And Lucas had agreed. It would be better that way. No chance of Cary's wandering eye wandering in a way that would hurt him and foul their financial interests.

When Cary's attention was on him, it was like laying in the sun. But he knew what it was like when the sun went away. And it hurt more than Lucas wanted to examine. Ever.

Hoping to stave off complicated emotions, he fixed his

attention on Francesca. If she was going to join them for the weekend, he might as well learn as much about her as he could right now. Before Cary stole her wits with kisses and the other wicked games he undoubtedly planned to play with her.

"Ted is an idiot." He knew he was repeating himself, but he wanted her to know that. She was beautiful—glossy brown waves and freckled brown skin, framed by a lush mouth and brown-green eyes. His palms itched to move over the subtle curves of her body. His mind flashed to her naked beneath his hands, still while he took his time learning each nook and cranny of her. He wanted to touch her, and he wanted to protect her. Both things at once.

And then he wanted to fuck her until she looked at him with the same heat she gave Cary. It was jealousy, but not jealousy that made him want her all to himself. He couldn't explain it, but he just wanted what Cary had with her.

Cary could watch from his arm chair with a satisfied smile on his face, glass of scotch dangling from his fingertips before he joined them on bed. His erstwhile lover enjoyed a show. He'd always surrounded himself with hedonic pleasures and luxury. Cary was all about expensive fabric, fine food, and special-occasion champagne for breakfast. He was flash and fire, but intense and single-minded about what he wanted.

The way he licked his lips told Lucas that his single-minded focus was split in that moment.

"That's very nice of you to say," Francesca lowered her gaze to her new re-filled glass. "But I think Ted knew what I wouldn't admit to myself."

"And what's that?" Cary asked.

"Grams is sick." Lucas was lost, so he did what he did best—listened. "And I wanted to surprise her with an engagement over Christmas, but it was stupid." She shook her head. "I didn't want to be Ted's wife."

She was ready to get engaged just to make her grand-mother happy? No one in his family would sacrifice a dram of whisky for him, but she was willing to tie her life to a man of average intelligence, just to make her grandmother happy? No wonder Cary was so tied up about her. One thing they had in common was an alarming level of disloyalty from their relations. It was one of the reasons they'd always been loyal friends to each other even though they'd never been exclusive sexually. They both needed someone, some-thing steadfast in their lives. They'd been that too each other.

But Francesca was something else entirely. Francesca's fierce commitment to making a sick old woman happy would throw them both for a loop. It made Lucas want to pull the ripcord on Cary's whole—still unarticulated—plan. This woman had the potential to throw off their delicate balance. He could see the way she affected Cary. He shifted in his hair and pulled at his collar. His never-ruffled friend was appearing discombobulated by her. And if she could Cary into a school boy, he was completed fucked.

Hell, he was fucked the moment she turned her gaze on him and changed the subject. "How long have you known this one?"

"Decades." Lucas cleared his throat. It was already start-ing. "We met a uni."

She laughed, and it grabbed him by the root of his cock. "I'll bet he was a handful even back then."

"I'll have you know that I've always been two handfuls."

No mistaking the flush on her chest with the reference to Cary's cock. Only remained to be seen how she felt about the other cock in the equation. "Can you believe the cheek of this one?" Dear lord, she was even charming when making fun of their accents.

"Never could." His face muscles formed a smile, in spite of his reticence. He wanted this woman even more than he'd wanted to escape into Cary's den of sin for the week before going back to London to tie up the rest of his affairs.

He looked over at Cary, and his friend saw all the things that Lucas wanted. That's what Cary did—saw everything, read minds, moved chess pieces, and gave pleasure. It was always amazing to be with him but devastating when he decided to take it all away. But he wasn't taking it all away quite yet. If Francesca was amenable, they could have tonight.

"Francesca, love, why don't you come back to ours for a night cap?"

3

———

Having two men flirt with her mere minutes after being dumped sure was a boon for her confidence. *They were flirting with her, right?* Despite the fact that she felt like they were both focused completely on her, in completely prurient ways, she couldn't help but wonder what their deal was. They seemed to have an unspoken way of conversing with their eyes. And, for some reason, it really turned her on.

And, given her previous relationship with Cary, she knew that his invitation for a nightcap meant more than a drink or two. It meant a tumble back into Cary's bed. But did it mean something would happen with Lucas. She'd only just met him, but the moment his hand had engulfed hers, her whole body had gone hot and molten.

His piercing blue eyes seared her insides and made her want to kneel at his feet. She and Cary had played sexy games together, but nothing extreme or formal. That just wasn't his way. Cary was a man used to being in charge, used to being obeyed. She was a woman who obeyed no man.

When they'd come together, it had been a teeth-gnashing fight for dominance, but she'd always given it up for him eventually. It was much more pleasurable for both of them that way.

And he'd always appreciated her frankness. "Are we talking about drinking and talking, or are you hoping to get your dick wet?"

Cary laughed out loud. "I forgot how direct you are."

"That's not an answer." She wasn't about to leave this restaurant without knowing what was on the table. She had a plane to catch the following morning and coming out of baggage claim looking thoroughly fucked would raise questions from the cousin picking her up. Questions she was not prepared to answer. "And I have a plane to catch in the morning."

"What do you want to happen?" Lucas' question took her off guard. She'd already gleaned that he was a quiet man who didn't waste words. Not only did she appreciate that in light of Ted's affinity for the sound of his own voice, but it added to the whole mysterious badass thing that he had going on. If they were serious about fucking her tonight, it would be a glorious. She could get her rebound in before flying home.

She leaned towards him, meeting his gaze and letting him get a glimpse down her shirt. "It depends on what's on the table. Both of you seem to be flirting with me and you have a—connection, clearly."

Cutting against her mysterious badass theory about Lucas, his cheeks colored.

"What do you want to be on the table, love?" Cary wouldn't let himself be forgotten. "If Lucas and I had our druthers, you'd be spread out on this table here for dessert."

It was her turn to feel her skin heat and lava pool in her panties. If one of them touched her right now, she would probably go up like a pile of dry kindling. She'd fantasized about two men, read books. She'd even told Cary that being the focus of two men sounded sexy, but she hadn't vocalized that she would never think to do it. Not many men she'd met wanted to share or had fluid enough sexuality to cross swords and not be weird about it.

Still, given the circumstances, spending the night hot, sweaty, and naked might not be the worst way to work the adrenaline of her very recent break up out of her muscles. She knew from experience that Cary's kisses were like a drug. Even remembering them had her lips tingling. And he was telling her that she could have that—plus Lucas?

All she could think of was being spread across Cary's giant glass desk in his home office, him kissing her mouth as Lucas' dark head dipped between her thighs.

She wanted that. Just a few hours, and she'd be able to think about that instead of the fact that her grandmother would look at her as though she couldn't remember her this year and then really forget her by the next. It was probably fool-hardy, but after losing what she'd thought was a safe bet in Ted, she craved a bit of risk.

But first, she needed answers. She motioned between the two men. "Seriously, what's your deal? Are you boyfriends? Lovers? Just friends who want to get their freak on because the Christmas is just so unbearably sexy?"

Cary smiled, and Lucas grimaced. "We're old friends." Cary shrugged nonchalantly, but she knew him well enough to know that he did nothing without a purpose. "Sometimes more."

"Have you had threesomes with other women?" Frankie

was not acting out of jealousy. She wanted to know if this was going to be so awkward that it would ruin her fantasy, or if they would make it worth the lost sleep.

"We have." She trusted Lucas' solemn declaration.

"And you're on board with this?" It would be shitty of her to crash their—whatever—if Lucas wasn't into it. He might have been all about flirting, but maybe he came all the way from the UK to have Cary's mouth to himself. She wouldn't blame him at all for that.

He nodded and shocked her when he took her hand in his again. Again, the contact was a jolt to her system, continuing her danger of overheating. He was just as potent a drug as Cary, and he hadn't even kissed her yet. She couldn't take her gaze off the way the muscles of his forearms flexed as he moved his fingers up her bare arm.

"So soft."

She might have moaned out loud with his low, gruff words. But she didn't have time to analyze it because Cary cupped the side of her neck and snagged her attention again.

"The staff's drinking the wine I bought them in back." That was her only warning before he took her mouth with his.

Everything.

Being kissed by Cary George was everything. At first glance, he might have seemed mild-mannered and professorial, but that impression had evaporated the first time he'd kissed her. And the swipe of his tongue melted all of her internal misgivings about taking whatever adventure he'd planned for the night as soon as they'd locked gazes across this room. She would never be strong enough to pass up kisses and more from this man.

And having another man's fingers crawl up her arm, the dry, callused tips rubbing across her exposed collarbone until she was moaning into Cary's mouth. Feeling Lucas' gaze on them both heightened the whole of it.

She was more turned on right then than she had been the last time she'd had sex with Ted. Not that he was bad, but this was a fantasy come to life.

Cary broke the kiss even though she would have happily kissed him all night. He pulled back, looking debauched in a way that made her want to eat his mouth for sustenance until she died of starvation. He'd always affected her, had always been deadly dangerous to let in.

"We should leave."

Frankie could only nod.

Lucas pulled her to her feet and didn't let her hand go right away. Dear lord, Lucas standing up was even better than Lucas brushing his fingers across her skin. Tall and broad, he looked as though he fought monsters for a living. Having spent enough time in the company of spies and knowing what she did about Cary's rather amorphous job description—fixer, lawyer, clean-up man—he probably killed monsters wearing people suits.

The idea of allowing her body—not her heart, she would never make that mistake with Cary again—open to these two men thrilled inside her. They were physically dangerous to bad men, but the only danger she was in would be dying from too much pleasure.

And that was definitely a risk she was willing to take.

CARY KEPT what Francesca had always called his "shit-eating grins" to a minimum as he retrieved her coat and called a car to the restaurant. If she thought he seemed too smug about her agreeing to go home with them, she'd probably slap him across the face. His Georgetown row house wasn't terribly far away, but she had on rather precarious footwear. It had started snowing, so a walk would be slow.

And he was anxious to have both of his dinner companions naked and summarily coming for him.

"Put the partition up." His plans for Francesca during the ride did not include an audience—outside of Lucas. He maneuvered her between them in the backseat of the town car. She didn't protest, but he could feel her ire. Sweet, tart Francesca hated being maneuvered. But she so liked the results of his machinations that he knew she would love it when he lifted the bottom of her skirt and whispered, "Be a good girl," in her ear.

She didn't brush his hands away, just smiled at him with too many teeth.

"How did you meet this bossy arse?" Lucas had the best timing when asking questions. It would be lovely to play with Francesca's cunt during the short ride to his home— when she couldn't make any of the noise he knew he could draw from her. And Lucas was game to play along by the way he ignored Cary's hand journeying up Francesca's lean, strong thigh.

This was indulgent, but Cary never had been one to deny himself. Francesca made his cock so hard that he felt the need to punish her for it. She made a clawing desire come awake in his belly whenever he set eyes on her. He'd taken to avoiding a certain cable news channel that she appeared on as a contributor. Explaining why U.S. domestic policy made his cock hard in his conference room was not one of his goals.

"We met through work." Her vague answer wouldn't satisfy Lucas, but Cary appreciated her discretion. His professional interests were varied, and not always the right side of legal. Lucas knew this. And he knew that Cary always did the right thing, regardless of whether it conformed to the letter of the law. "I'm not sure what he was doing at that cocktail party, he wasn't on the invite list."

Lucas laughed, the rough, harsh sound a turn on. "He never waits for an invitation, he barrels right in."

Francesca looked at him then, meeting his gaze. What he saw in her eyes crystalized what he wanted from her. He wanted everything. Even though he didn't know if he could handle everything, if he could make her happy, seeing her again made him realize that he wanted to try. "It's just that he knows he's welcome everywhere he wants to go—at least tonight."

Cary's fingers found her lacy panties covering her mons, and Lucas dipped his head towards her neck. He couldn't be sure why her head hit the seatback with the degree of force it did, whether it was him rubbing her pussy or Lucas nibbling on her ear but touching her felt right—more right than anything he'd experienced since parting ways with Francesca last year.

He wanted to pull her over his lap, move that infuriating panel of lace to the side, and thrust deep inside her. Her ferocious confidence and the vulnerability that she only showed those who earned her trust. It was intoxicating. She was intoxicating—more than any wine or rotgut, bathtub gin.

Instead of letting his control snap and devouring her in the car, he satisfied himself with rubbing her until she writhed against his hand and moaned into Lucas' mouth. Hearing his best friend eat those sounds made him feel almost—peaceful. As though perhaps he could be enough for both of them when he wasn't enough for either on his own.

That was all they had time for before the car rolled to a stop in front of his home.

4

———

Francesca kissed like a dream and had him as hard as a rock, but Lucas had never been less sure of anything than he was of what they were about to do once they crossed the threshold into Cary's house.

His best friend had always been able to make decisions on a dime, the first to sign on to a prank at school, and the one who'd seduced the other partners they'd shared. Back when Lucas hadn't been sure why he was so drawn to Cary in particular, Cary had been the one to suggest they snog and find out what it was about. But, rushing in to possibly disastrous experiments had never been Lucas' way. He was all about the careful, strategic plodding to the right conclusion. Unless he could see how things would end, he never dove in.

But with Francesca sitting between them in the car, he hadn't been able to stop himself from kissing her. Especially when she asked so nicely. On a gasp from Cary's hands working between her legs in the car's dark interior.

And now, watching her truly magnificent ass sway as she picked her way up the steps into Cary's row house. He was hypnotized by the movement. So much so that he thought he was probably going mad.

Never a believer in love at first sight, or even in the idea of falling in love in general, he wondered if that was what was happening to him now. He'd never been quite so smitten quite so quickly. It made his head swim, and that couldn't be good. If it lasted past their night together, it could put his and Cary's lives in danger.

Good thing it was only one night.

He must not have been moving quickly enough because Cary stared at him from just inside the door. "Are you going to dawdle out there all night?"

Lucas shook his head and ran up the stairs into the interior of his friend's home—his home for the next little while until he figured out whether he could really leave his life in London behind for good. Until he sussed out whether he could just work with the man he was so attached to. Whether that attachment would fade or drive him absolutely mad.

As he crossed the threshold, Cary snagged his forearm and moved him until they were facing each other. Lucas could feel Francesca's attention on his back.

"Head to the study, love," Cary said. "Pour us all drinks so that we can have a chat before proceeding."

Francesca sniffed, probably gave Cary and one-fingered salute, but her heels echoed away from them through the corridor.

"Are you sure we should do this?" Even as he asked the question, he knew that Cary was sure. He'd always been sure of everything—that women and the occasional man would fall at his feet, eager to meet his whims, that his family money would pad his fall wherever he landed, that none of his debauchery would ever hurt his reputation.

And, indeed, tales of his exploits had only made people who wanted to hire him to clean up *their* indiscretions were only ever intrigued. "I mean, you and she seem to have quite a bit of history, and I don't want to insert myself."

Truth told, he wanted nothing more. He wanted the three of them together, and he wanted it now.

Cary smiled, and the gleam of it struck Lucas like it always had. They were close enough that the earthy, clean smell of Cary's skin burned Lucas' nostrils—as though he'd imprinted on the ginger charmer the instant he'd turned all of that golden attention on him. "You definitely want to insert yourself, and I wouldn't have invited you if I didn't know her quite so well."

"What do you mean?"

"You and me together is everything she's ever wanted." Cary stepped closer and put his hand inside Lucas's jacket. "I've never felt a woman come so hard as when I told her about that time in Paris after we finished school while I fucked her from behind."

"But that was a fantasy—"

"And this is reality."

They locked gazes, and Lucas knew he was going to do whatever Cary wanted. Years of bucking orders from everyone above him in Her Majesty's service, but he couldn't say no to Cary. That was beyond his ken.

MAYBE LUCAS WASN'T into her? That had to be what they were talking about in the lobby. He'd certainly seemed like he was on board when he'd very expertly fucked her mouth with his in the cab, but that had just been a bit of heavy petting. Maybe he wanted Cary to himself and saw her as merely an opening act.

The whole thing made her doubt the decision to come here, even as she poured them all drinks. It was late. She had a flight to catch in the morning. But she didn't really want to face her family without a fiancé this year. And she could use a distraction from the dread that facing Grams' disapproval had lodged deep in her gut. She couldn't even fulfill the dying woman's wish to have her only single grand-child settled and happy. Frankie had convinced steel workers and stay-at-home moms to run for office in districts where their party hadn't won in decades, but she couldn't sell a candidate on being her husband—or even her fake fiancé for two weeks. She was like a shoeless cobbler that couldn't find the right fit.

Dammit, Ted.

Cary and Lucas entering the room pushed all thoughts about her failed campaign to become affianced out of her head. They were simply too hot to entertain thoughts of failure and looking at her as though she was an oasis in the desert.

It almost hurt to look at them; she had to look away and contemplate the flakes of snow reflected in the street light, falling to the pavement outside. Just a flurry. Shouldn't cause too much travel chaos. But this was D.C., so she'd have to be at the airport early in any event.

Best to get this show on the road, then. "You boys sort everything out?"

Cary smiled, and Lucas grimaced, dialing back her confidence level by several notches. Maybe her doubts had been telling her something?

"We haven't gotten you sorted out, love." She loved the way the rough burr of Lucas' voice stroked over the endearment. She'd like it even more if he said it in the curve of her neck as he pounded into her from behind.

Jesus, they were liable to turn her into a sex maniac if she wasn't careful. She could easily see herself becoming addicted to the two of them together, much the same way that she'd gone into withdrawal after things broke off with Cary.

And maybe that was all that Ted was—something low dose to get over the thing she really wanted.

But she was over Cary now, and knew the score. To prove it, she'd have this conversation, and walk out the front door and into her uncertain future after wringing as many orgasms out of the experience as possible. "What needs sorting out? I thought we'd taken care of any sorting in the cab?"

Lucas finally broke a smile. "But I don't know—for sure —what you want from all this."

"I thought we'd gone over that in uni," Cary said as he handed his friend a drink. "You know, Tab A, Slot B."

"As long as you don't forget to ring the doorbell before you enter, I'm sure we'll get along just fine." Frankie's sarcastic sense of humor was one of her best qualities, but it was also her most effective defense mechanism. She tended to joke about the things she felt vulnerable about, and Cary knew that. The look he gave her told her that he knew that was what she was doing now.

But then he rounded the enormous kitchen island and moved his tall, sinewy body behind her. He was going to let her get away with it this once because he wanted to fuck her as much as he'd wanted to the night she'd left him hard and confused in his bed upstairs a year ago. As long as she could remind herself that this was just for the night, she would walk out the door without a broken heart this time.

"Tell Lucas what you want." Cary ran his lips over the place where her shoulder and neck met. Just the spot to turn her brainless—exactly what she needed in that moment. "He won't do anything until he knows that you want everything we have planned for you."

She met Lucas' intense blue gaze and smiled at him. "I want everything you have planned for me."

The corner of his mouth turned up. "Show me."

"How so?" She raised one brow—a feat given that Cary started kissing and licking the skin at the back of her neck, almost buckling her knees.

Lucas removed onyx cufflinks and set them on the marble counter. Cary had her hemmed in across from him, his cock rubbing her lower back through their clothes, his tongue tracing wicked plans against her skin. She was shivering hot, a mess. But when Lucas rolled up his sleeves, time seemed to stop. It was all she could do not to crawl over the counter and fall on his cock.

Lucas affected her more potently than any man except the one standing behind her. They were both devastating on their own. Together, surrounding her, they were apocalyptic.

She didn't have time to contemplate how they were going to obliterate her sanity because Cary's hand roamed over her side, up between her breasts coming to rest as he cupped her jaw. Possessive. He may not want to love her forever but wanted to know that she was his while they were together.

"Beautiful, isn't he?" She nodded in response, her movement jerky. "Brutal and deadly, but not when he's ours tonight."

Cary's nimble fingers moved so quickly that she was barely aware of him pulling her zipper down and unsticking the cups of her strapless, backless bra. "Clever that."

She didn't have a smartass remark for him then because he had both her nipples between his fingers and thumbs and Lucas was looking at her as though he hadn't just had dinner an hour ago. His hunger for her made her even wetter.

"Take your cock out and show her what she's going to have in her pretty mouth later." Something clicked into place. In that moment, she knew that—while Lucas might be big and rough and imposing—Cary would be the conductor of this whole symphony.

While Lucas followed their lover's instruction, Cary petted and stroked her body while peeling off the rest of her clothes until she was standing stark naked but for stockings and heels in the middle of his kitchen.

Cary came from a "posh" family that had connections to the Royal Family, but he'd never been afraid to say anything filthy that came to mind while they were fucking. Nothing that came out of his mouth should have shocked her, but she started when he tossed her panties at Lucas—who caught them—and said, "She's soaked them through. You should wrap them around your cock as you stroke it."

Lucas didn't miss a beat and wrapped one of his meaty hands—festooned with her panties—around his cock as Cary pushed his fingers in between her legs and rubbed her clit. She moaned, and it echoed off the vaulted ceilings.

"Shhh, love." Dear lord, he had her number, knew exactly what would make her moan more loudly. "If you keep that up, he'll come all over the kitchen floor."

Lucas grunted.

"I can't help it." Her voice had that breathy, Marilyn

Monroe quality that she hated, but knew spurred Cary on. "He's so much."

"Tell me what you want to do with it." Lucas looked down as though hearing her describe what she wanted would be too much for his delicate ears—even though the sight of him, clothed except for his dick with his hand and her lacy panties around it was not the filthiest thing anyone had ever seen in a kitchen.

"I want to suck it." Her words were a plea. "I want to taste myself all over it and swallow his come."

She couldn't stop looking at it. He was just so filthy and raw and open. It was too beautiful not to look at. But Cary had other ideas, he rubbed her clit faster and harder, exactly the way she liked until her eyes closed and an orgasm shimmered at the edges of her consciousness.

"Eyes open, love." She followed instructions and met Lucas' ruined gaze for a split second. And she was done. Her knees buckled, and she came with a scream. Her body bent over the counter, Cary covering her spine with kisses. "Just perfect. You're just perfect."

She turned her head just in time for Cary's mouth to cover hers again, devour her in a kiss. She wasn't sure how long it lasted but his kisses always felt as though they went on for a long while. But there was one problem—he wasn't naked or inside her, and Lucas hadn't come yet.

At some point, while she was coming, he'd rounded the counter. Still hard, but within her reach now. She reached out for him, but Cary took her hand and pulled her body upright, her back to his front. "I think it's time to put this one to bed, don't you?"

5

____

Lucas had never questioned Cary's taste in women, but Francesca was something else entirely. Utterly lovely, and likely the death of him. By the time they got to Cary's master bedroom, she was looking at his cock as though she'd never ridden Cary's fingers to orgasm.

"Do you want him to fuck you, love?" Cary was such an ass; he kept asking rhetorical questions when he knew very well that the vixen wanted just that. He shot his friend a look as he unbuttoned his shirt, revealing his scarred and used-up torso.

But she played along. "Very much."

"That's good, since I haven't even had a sip of this very fine whisky." Cary made a show of settling in one of the arm chairs facing the bed. As always, brimming with mischief and good humor. "Sit on the edge of the bed and suck his cock."

Francesca gave him the finger, which was dead sexy to Lucas, but she did as she was told. Then, she met his gaze and beckoned him with that same finger. She lit him up from the inside with that smart mouth. He barked out a laugh and lost his trousers as he moved toward her.

"You heard the man," he said, holding his cock out of her to take. He hesitated for a brief moment. "But only if you want to."

She bit her bottom lip, and he couldn't help reaching out and freeing that plump flesh from her teeth. He looked down her whole body, taking in the plump little breasts and hard dusky nipples, the mostly flat belly still slick with sweat from their interlude in the kitchen. Then, he met her molten gaze.

"I want to." She bent her head and took him inside her mouth. He groaned and laced his fingers through her hair, not to push her head, but to have a hold on her so that she couldn't devour him whole and steal his come before he was ready.

From behind him, he heard Cary's clothes ruffle, knowing that he wouldn't be able to hold off touching himself watching this. He'd always liked to watch.

"Fuck, love, that's good."

She made him delirious—a thousand different images of gloriously filthy things he wanted to do to her. Far too many for the one night they had. Because, even though he didn't know her well at all, he'd seen the steel in her spine and the shutters in her gaze before Cary had stripped and finger-fucked her in the kitchen. She wanted this to be just sex, and he'd do his best to oblige, even though he wasn't sure he'd ever be able to touch his cock again without thinking of her screaming and coming all over Cary's hand. Everything she gave him made him want more of her.

The sight of them together had been almost enough to make him blow. Almost as much as her mouth was doing to him now.

"Enough." He pulled her away, growled at the sight of her swollen and bright red lips, and turned to Cary. "Where do you keep the condoms?"

SOMETHING ABOUT LUCAS had set her on fire, and she wasn't bothered to find out what it was before it burned out. It didn't matter why she'd been so turned on by sucking him off that she'd been rocking her hips against the duvet. She'd probably nearly come all over bedding that cost more of her condo payment, but she knew that Cary wouldn't care.

"In the side table." Cary pointed with his rocks glass, masterful grin firmly in place. She wondered what it would take for him to lose it and go feral in the same way that Lucas had when she'd licked the underside of the tip of his cock. That maneuver had never made Cary growl and go wild. He'd simply smiled and asked her whether she'd wanted him to fuck her face.

She had.

"Are you going to join us, or just sit there watching like a perv?" He liked it when she goaded him. Something about growing up in a house with bowing servants, living in a world where everyone was expected to follow orders, made him like it when she told him what was what.

"I'm going to, as you so eloquently put it, sit here like a perv and watch Lucas fuck you until you scream."

Lucas was in front of her then, with a smile on his face that echoed Cary's—cocky. "You, too?"

His brow furrowed. "What? I like hearing you talk back to him."

"Both so cocky..." And she liked it so much—too much.

Her gaze snagged down to that particular appendage as

she spoke. He stroked it, and it was so lurid that she lost the will to talk back.

"Scoot back, love." He put on the condom. "You know how His Grace hates it when his supplicants don't follow orders."

She did it because she wanted his cock inside her more than she wanted her next breath. She wanted him to fuck her more than she'd wanted her first job, more than she'd ever wanted Ted to win his congressional seat. More than anything.

She laid back and luxuriated in letting him look at her. She liked her body, and he liked knowing that he liked it too. He surprised her, though. She expected him to position his big body over hers and thrust inside. And she almost wanted him to do it. To rut and grunt and remind her that she wasn't meant to be a nearly sexless trophy wife for an empty suit for the rest of her life.

Instead, he ran his fingers over her belly, the rough sensation making her gasp. And she caught Cary's breath catching from the other side of the room.

This is where she would usually throw off a smart remark to Cary, who liked the meandering road to orgasms. She was greedy and wanted more. More would be good right now, but she had the feeling that Lucas needed this—a moment. And she just might need it too.

"Gorgeous." Yeah, giving him a moment was totally worth it. His fingertips moved over her mons, and he gave her clit a rub that made her whole body jerk. Her arms flew over her head. "Thrust your pretty tits up."

Jesus, did they each know how to dirty talk or what? "Please."

"Please what?" His filthy smile came back, and she didn't

know if she liked that more than the wildlife documentary level snarling.

"Fuck me."

She gasped and arced higher when he thrust a finger deep inside her, positioning his thumb on her clit to keep up the friction.

"Is that good, love?"

"You know," she gasped. "Damn well it is."

"Always so much cheek from this one." That came from Cary, who stroked his cock from the chair, his face growing a bit red and hair mussed. This was affecting him after all, which turned her on even more than she'd ever thought possible. "I'd nearly forgotten how much I like getting heckled by my bed partner."

Lucas grinned. "I don't know, I liked it when her mouth was otherwise occupied."

It shouldn't turn her on for them to be talking about her as though she wasn't there. As though she was an object. But she rather enjoyed being an object of their desire—as though they were using her to get off and that the real thing was between them. It felt safer than anything she'd ever had with Cary on their own. That had always had a lot of edge to it. The two of them alone had a volatile dynamic—not physically—just that they would poke at each other until one of them walked out of the room in a huff or fucked like minks on the dining room table.

There was something about Lucas' long-standing relationship with Cary, his steady presence, that stabilized both her and Cary. She liked it. Probably too much.

She didn't have time to think on it too much because Lucas stretched his body over hers, touching her almost everywhere and replacing his fingers with his cock at her gate. For just a moment, no one in the room could breathe.

She didn't like to place that much importance on penis-in-vagina sex as the point of sex. After all, they'd been having sex for the better part of the hour, but this felt more intimate than even having his cock in her mouth.

Missionary sex, face-to-face with a man who'd been a stranger a few hours ago. Who didn't feel like a stranger at all.

She drank in the scent of whisky on his breath, the way his skin threw off pheromones that her body ate up. Before thinking on it, she dug her fingers into his hair, scraping his scalp with her nails.

And he purred into her mouth as she kissed him, and he thrust inside her. He filled her up—more than just his cock, it was as though his essence filled her skin, and she would never be the same. She couldn't possibly be the same after this.

"Fuck." His rough voice betrayed that he was affected by this as well.

He pulled back, and she nearly mewled. She would mutiny if he didn't keep fucking her, but she didn't know what the threesome protocol was. Did he only get a limited number of thrusts before Cary would get to take over?

That made her laugh, and it made Lucas stop. "Something funny, love?"

She sobered. The way he was looking intently at her made the idea that he wasn't completely focused on what was happening in this bed seem crazy. "I've never done this before."

"Are you still okay with this?" He stayed still even though she could feel the strain in his shoulder muscles from doing so.

"More than okay." She canted her hips. "Please."

"Please what, love?" Cary said from the corner, his voice

sounding as strained as Lucas' ability to control himself was. "You have to be very clear with him."

Lucas snarled at that.

"Please fuck me, Lucas."

And, for the first time that night, Lucas followed her instructions. It didn't last long, just like this couldn't possibly last long. They'd been playing for what seemed like hours, and he had to be on a hair trigger, just an instant from coming at any moment.

"Touch yourself, love." He grunted. "Need to see you come again."

She disengaged one hand from Lucas' sweat-dampened hair and rubbed her clit in time with his thrusts. It was seconds before she was flying, her legs wrapped around Lucas' hips as he finally let himself lose control and fuck her through an orgasm that left her mindless and boneless, desperate to keep him inside her, but needing to crawl into a dark corner and shut the world off until it settled back on its axis.

His hips jerked one last time, and she didn't know why she met his gaze in that moment. All she knew was that something about the world had rearranged while they came together. Something that ought to have terrified her.

6

———

Cary didn't like to feel like he was on the outside looking in. He liked to be in the thick of things—smashing dictatorships, winning elections, making sure that the truly corrupt didn't wrest power from the hands of those truly deserving. But he liked to do it from atop the perch he'd built for himself. Nothing could touch him there, break open his chest and rip out the contents.

When he saw the way that Lucas looked at Francesca as she slept, he finally figured out why he'd broken things off with her a year ago. She'd been such a danger to his precious fucking perch that he hadn't had a choice. Had he kept seeing her, he would have fallen in love with her. He would have been walking around with his ribcage wide open, all of his innards vulnerable to the world. And that just wouldn't do.

He was almost thankful that Lucas had fucked her into a stupor. Had her ravenous desire, which he loved, been turned on him, he wouldn't have been able to resist. He would have been inside her as soon as she turned those flashing hazel eyes on him. And he would have been lost.

As it was, he was almost lost watching the way that Lucas had her tucked into his side. He'd never seen his friend want to keep a woman around after he'd played with her. Lucas was the only person Cary knew who was as closed off as he was. It was why they'd been able to stay close friends for so long, the reason that they could work together, that they could fuck each other and then not be in the same city for months, the reason that Lucas was the only person he'd ever take on as a business partner. The reason that Lucas was the only person he trusted.

They fit together. But Francesca showing up at that restaurant had thrown both of them for a loop. Before, when they'd shared, it had been almost choreographed. But this was entirely new. Cary had chemistry with both Lucas and Francesca—them together had been nuclear.

And Cary wasn't certain whether he liked being left out of that.

So, he cleaned his hand with a cloth handkerchief and tucked himself back into his pants—he'd come when they had because they'd been too beautiful together not to. He stalked over to the bed and sat down with his back propped up on the headboard on Francesca's other side. Between them. She fit between them.

He would have moved then, but she shifted in her sleep and wrapped her hand over his thigh. Lucas looked down at where she touched him. "This is why nothing happened in Nairobi last year?"

The one time he'd seen Lucas while he and Francesca had been dating, they hadn't fucked. And Lucas had been hurt, but Cary had felt as though it would have been a betrayal. Christ, he should have known then that Francesca as trouble.

Cary nodded, needing to shut down the train before it pulled into Feelings Town. "This doesn't change anything."

"Changes everything, and you know it." Lucas wasn't one to lie to anyone—including himself. "I want her."

"You've just fucked her, and I'm sure she'll be up for fucking again once she has a few minutes of sleep." He instantly felt guilty for insinuating that this was just sex, and that he had no idea that Lucas was talking about more than their mutual pleasure. His friend wasn't the type of man who hesitated to meet his own needs. If he'd decided that those needs included Francesca in his bed, he would move mountains to have that.

Although he was as closed off to the outside world as he was, once someone was in his circle of protection, they were in. The way his entire body curved around the sleeping woman between them, the way the rest of the world had disappeared when they'd fucked, told Cary that Francesca was firmly ensconced in the circle.

But all of this complicated things immensely. Would Lucas and Francesca want Cary to play with them? Or would they want him as a permanent fixture in their relationship? He'd fouled things up too severely with Francesca for her to trust him with her heart again—he was sure of it. If she wanted him at all, it would only be for sex.

And this made his standing with Lucas much less clear as well. If he and Francesca were together, it would be easier to keep Lucas in D.C. But if they were all fucking, Lucas may not want to be business partners after all. He liked to keep things neat and compartmentalized. A threesome with his business associate and his ex-girlfriend could be quite messy.

Lucas seemed to sense Cary's turbulent thoughts. He cupped his chin and pulled his face close. Fuck, he smelled

Francesca all over him, and he was turned on again. But this wasn't about his cock at the moment, it was about his life. His best friend and the only woman who had ever threatened him with love.

"We'll work it out in the morning." Lucas said, before kissing the corner of his mouth. "I can see your mind turning."

"She'll be gone in the morning." Cary couldn't help smooth a strand behind her ear, she snuffled, but kept as much of her back flush with Lucas' side and her hand gripped Cary's thigh. "Back home to her family."

Lucas inclined his chin toward the window. Snow fell outside at a decidedly fast clip. "No one is getting out of National tomorrow."

Cary felt the truth of that settle into him. He wanted more time. Hell, he wanted the chance to fuck Francesca again. Maybe that would finally cure him of her and any wild ideas of making a life with both her and Lucas. He'd resigned himself a few more hours, but a few more days would be even better.

"So, she'll stay." The idea of spending Christmas with them both settled into his bones, as though it had been the plan all along. "She's going to be pissed."

Lucas just grunted as though that didn't worry him at all. But he'd never seen Francesca angry. He would love it.

7

—————

Francesca didn't know where she was when she woke up, which hadn't happened since college. Come to think of it, she'd been naked and sore between her legs back then too. The main difference was that, back in college, she'd been very cold and in her boyfriend's trash bedroom at a frat house.

She was anything but cold in the moment, facing a well-pelted chest and Lucas' sleeping visage. Memories of how he'd gently tucked her under Cary's very expensive sheets after fucking her until she could barely see rushed her. She shifted her legs, setting off a zing—just a hint—of the pleasure that he'd given her last night. Before she'd closed her eyes, the last thing she remembered was Cary cleaning come off of his hand—measured and efficient—and looking at her with his intense and inscrutable gaze.

Although she was fine with what went down the night before, she hadn't expected it to be so intense. Fun, yes. Earth-shattering, no.

And she hadn't expected Lucas to stay curled around her

body as she slept. She'd expected him to creep out the bedroom before she was fully asleep.

The other primary problem was that it was light outside, and her flight had left before sunrise. That thought had her jerking up in bed, gooseflesh covering her where the duvet had been.

"Fuck."

Lucas stirred and rubbed a hand down his face. The night before, he'd been an almost-frightening fuck beast, but this morning he was almost cute. "What is it?"

"I missed my flight."

He had the nerve to smile at her. Perhaps it wasn't such a big deal for him to miss out on the holidays with his family. Clearly not, because he was spending the most wonderful time of the year balls deep inside his best friend's ex-girlfriend.

That pissed her off, so she shook his shoulder just as he looked like he was going to re-settle himself under the covers. Under other circumstances, it might even be cute. But she was going to have to try to change her flight after missing the first one, which she knew the airline would give her a rasher of shit about—even given her double-platinum diamond status from her work. And that was even if there was room on a flight. In all likelihood, she would end up waking up on Christmas morning in the first-class lounge.

All because fucking Cary didn't see fit to wake her up as she'd asked him to in the event that she fell asleep after fucking him one last time—which she hadn't even done.

She ripped the duvet off her body and searched the room for her clothes, ready to tear Cary a new asshole before a Christmas Eve Uber of shame back to her U Street condo. But she didn't get very far because Lucas grabbed her wrist.

When she looked down at his face, the deadly serious thing was back. "Go easy."

"Pfft." She had no intention of doing that. This wasn't about Lucas at all—he'd been in between her and Cary last night for a reason. Just the two of them was a tinderbox ready to explode at any moment. "Whatever."

She wrenched her hand out of his grip and found his t-shirt. Would have to do for murdering Cary. And it would save her from getting his blue blood all over her clothes. And then, in a stroke of genius, she shoved her feet into the shearling slippers laid out by the door.

As she stomped down the stairs to make sure that Cary would hear her from the kitchen, she could have let her temper cool down. But she wouldn't let herself do that. If she didn't make it home for Christmas, she'd lose her last holiday with her grandmother, the woman who had helped raise her into the woman she was now. Whether she liked the results or not.

Cary was making coffee, something he had never done during their short affair. In fact, he'd often wanted her out of his home after fucking her—early meetings with important people and all that. That's why it perplexed her so much that he'd simply forget to wake her up in time for her to catch her flight.

When she reached the kitchen he turned, and she was momentarily stunned. Even though the old house had a chill, he wasn't wearing a shirt. Her gaze snagged on a trail of dark red hair that lead into some red and black flannel pajama bottoms that did nothing to hide his semi-hard cock.

What had he been thinking about while making coffee?

"Black, right?" She met his eyes then, his face trained to appear noncommittal.

That pissed her off. She put her hands on her hips, not

paying attention to the fact that it hiked the t-shirt up enough that he could probably see her hoo-ha. "I missed my flight."

She walked further into the kitchen when he pushed a mug across the island—the one he'd held her against while fingering her the night before.

"Your flight was cancelled."

"But you could have woken me up to tell me that."

"And deliberately upset you?" He smiled, and she wanted to slap him across the face. "When I could do it by accident so much more easily? I know how you are with very little sleep."

He was referring to the night they'd met. She had been at a cocktail party in the Hay-Adams hotel, waiting for a client to show up. It had been the last place she'd wanted to be because she'd pulled two all-nighters in a row getting an unsuccessful presentation ready.

To top off her shit sandwich of a week, her client hadn't shown up—sending Cary instead. She'd heard whispers of the man for years, and seen him in passing, but never had his full attention turned on her.

He'd said, "You don't look nearly as formidable as I expected," and sat down, unbuttoning the jacket on his bespoke suit. That alone had pissed her off enough that she'd thrown her martini in his face and stalked off.

Everything had been patched up when he'd sent a spray of exotic wildflowers and a check from the client to compensate her for her time. A dinner invitation had followed, and she'd accepted in hopes of preventing him from spreading rumors that she was an incompetent hothead all over town. It was just him and that thing he did when he smiled at her.

The rest was sordid history that she didn't want to revisit. If she was going to be stuck with him and Lucas for the day, she didn't want to be thinking about how she'd fallen in love with Cary. She couldn't spend the whole time reliving how stupid she'd been.

"You're not going to throw hot coffee in my face, are you?" He'd always had a way of knowing what she was thinking, even though her poker face was nearly foolproof for anyone but him. "Would sting a bit more than gin and vermouth."

"Shut up." She took the coffee and blew on the top. Then, she looked up and caught Cary's attention on her mouth. "Why didn't you tell me that there was a storm coming in?"

He pushed her phone across the island. There was a notification from shortly after she'd gone to sleep that her flight had been cancelled and she should call the airline for re-booking. "You've been responsible for yourself for a long time, love." He shrugged, and she admired the way that his muscles and bones shifted under his skin. "I figured I'd let you sort it out yourself."

She'd been distracted by the idea that she was going to get engaged the night before. Her mind had skipped over the whole "make sure that a snowpocalypse wasn't about to befall the D.C. metro area" and skipped right to "I hope my hair cooperates and my engagement ring is very large and sparkly."

If she'd known how last night would go, she wouldn't be here now. She'd have gotten the getting dumped over with much earlier the day before and caught an early flight, during which she would have come up with a good cover story for why Ted wasn't with her.

She sighed and caught Cary's mouth tip up at one side. He must love this, given how much he enjoyed stymieing her plans—for her career, for their relationship, and now for getting home for Christmas.

"We still have power, which means coffee—" He tipped up his mug. "And we'll have a hot Christmas dinner."

A rush of anxiety filled her belly as she rushed over to the window. Snow had piled to seats of the wrought iron chairs on his patio, and the snow continued to fall in fat, white flakes. Or splatted and turned into water against the window, obscuring her view.

"How long is it supposed to snow?" She looked over her shoulder at him, unable to keep her belly from heating at the sight as he took a sip of coffee. "A few hours?"

He winced. "More like a few days, love."

"A few days!?" She knew she sounded like a shrieking banshee, but it never snowed in D.C. for a few days. The last time it had happened, everything had shut down for at least a week. No planes had landed at National or left, and the shelves at grocery stores had been stripped bare. And that hadn't even been during the busiest travel week of the year.

This was a disaster. Missing Christmas with her family —as imperfect as they were—would be especially painful this year. She was meant to say goodbye to the grandmother who'd helped raise her. She wanted to give her good news and let her drift away thinking that Frankie had finally found the kind of happiness and fulfillment she'd wanted for her.

Even if the happiness and fulfillment had been a temporary fib.

"What is it?" Cary moved closer to her, close enough that she could feel the heat of his body. Part of her wanted to shift away, run and hide under the covers next to Lucas. He seemed safe because all they had between them was scorching hot sex. She and Cary had way too much history for him to ever be her safe place. He could never be her home again.

But she didn't want to give him the satisfaction of knowing how much he affected her still—at least not outside of how much she enjoyed his tall, rangy body giving her pleasure.

"My grandmother is sick." She paused, not sure if she should give Cary the whole story knowing that he might see fit to use it against her. She weighed his Machiavellian nature against his often magnanimous need to fix things for her. Like the time he'd somehow summoned a helicopter to get to a client's campaign event because he'd made her so late. "She's not going to be the same even a few months from now, and I'd wanted her to know I was engaged before she's gone."

Cary's lips thinned to a hard line. He couldn't possibly be angry at the thought of her engaged to someone else? That was totally ridiculous, given that he'd broken up with her because he couldn't commit. He did not get to be jealous about this.

"Wipe that look off your face, Cary." She tried to use her most authoritative tone. "When and who I chose to marry is no longer any of your business."

"You certainly couldn't have meant to marry that bloody piece of shit who dumped you last night?"

Part of her really wanted to tell him the truth—that she wasn't entirely sure a wedding ever would have happened with Ted. But part of her wanted him to stew in his apparent jealousy. For once in their stormy relationship, she would have the upper hand.

"Why would you even care?"

~

WHY *WOULD* he care about whether she got engaged to some snot-nosed idiot?

For one thing, he still wanted her. But that wasn't enough for her to derail her whole life's plan for. He'd wanted he before, but he'd let her go because he had an iota of nobility in him. Even though he could never marry—her or anyone—he wasn't heartless enough to keep her on the string knowing that. He'd been honest about his intentions toward her, as much as it had gutted him.

For another thing, Ted wasn't good enough for her. It was plain as day. And even though he wasn't the sort to ever make a long-term commitment—seeing his parents' cold war-like marriage kill them both was enough to scare him off the whole concept—he didn't want Francesca to tie herself to someone sub-par forever.

And, finally, he felt more alive with both Francesca and Lucas in his house than he had—well—since he'd done the right thing and broken things off with Francesca the year before.

The storm was serendipity, not that he quite believed in anything quite so ridiculous. He could spend a holiday with two people who made him feel whole and worthwhile when the whole world made him feel nothing but emptiness. The blizzard had delivered him a bit a grace for the holiday, and he wanted to hold onto it—just for a few days until it fell away.

Francesca's spine had lost a bit of its starch, so he took a chance and put his hand on her back. He stepped closer to her, close enough that their bodies touched. He liked her wearing his shirt, smelling of sex and Lucas. He wanted nothing more than to bury his nose as the crook of her neck, but he wasn't entirely sure she wouldn't deck him if he took the liberty.

"We still have internet, and we could Skype her." He offered, hoping that she would decline. It was selfish, but he wanted her and Lucas all to himself. Sharing with Lucas wasn't like sharing with her family, who he blamed for losing her in the first place. If her wretched grandmother hadn't made her believe she had to get married, they could have continued their affair until they'd had their fill of each other. He wouldn't have spent the entire last year aching and needing to jack off every time he thought of her. He wouldn't have felt like a pathetic, perverted schoolboy every time he'd taken himself in hand with a pair of her panties that he'd kept wrapped around his wrist.

"She doesn't use the internet—not since she got sick." He hated how defeated she sounded.

"You can go visit her next week?"

Francesca nodded, even though her disappointment was still a palpable thing between them. Still, he wanted to fix it for her. But even he, who had secrets of heads of state the world over at his fingertips, couldn't control the weather.

As usual, she surprised him and turned into his body. He wished that she were happy to be here, but he'd take her seeking comfort from him. Funny how greedy he felt about her even though he had no problem sharing her body with Lucas. He really hadn't ever had a problem sharing anything with Lucas, and the way Francesca fit between them made sense. When they'd first met, he'd thought how much Lucas would like Francesca—the way she laughed, the way she moved, her sharp mind and the way she chose her words so carefully until she was knocked off balance.

How fiercely she loved.

And that was it. She loved her grandmother enough to get engaged to a dunce of a man who couldn't see what a diamond he had in her. She loved so fiercely that she didn't hate Cary even though he'd—maybe—broken her heart.

So, he did all he could. He put down his mug, took hers from her shaky cold fingers, and held her close as she cried. Her tears chilled on his chest, and he wanted to somehow preserve them—wear them like a tattoo on his flesh even after she was gone.

He lost track of time while standing in his kitchen with her in his arms, he buried his face in her hair and made noises that he hoped were comforting. Her breathing slowed and became even. Finally, she pulled back and looked him in the face.

"You said there was food?"

8

"Plenty." Cary smiled at her. She didn't think they'd ever spent this much time in close contact without utilizing the nearest surface for some variety of sex act. It was weird to think about now, that she had decided she was in love with based on how hard and how often he made her come.

If her relationship with Ted had taught her anything, it was that a relationship couldn't be sustained on sex alone. But, with Ted, it had been all about her sustaining it for the both of them. Maybe next time, she'd be able to find a balance.

But, in that moment, she didn't care about the next guy. Or the guy after that. She only cared about the way that Cary was looking at her—his eyes without the customary twinkle. The look on his face and the way he'd held her told her that he would fix this for her, if he could. It was only his hard cock, poking into her belly through their clothes that told her that he was glad she was here.

The one thing she could do was put back the twinkle. She lifted herself up on tip-toe and pressed her lips to his.

He was still for a split second before he took over the kiss, eating her mouth with his. His hands, soothing just moments before, roamed up and down her back and pulled her flush against him. The heat of his flesh and muscle and bone pressed up against her breasts set her on fire.

She hadn't been kidding about being hungry before, but this was much more important. If she didn't have him inside her, she was pretty sure that she would die. Any hunger pangs burned away when she threaded her fingers through his hair and tugged his head down. He burrowed underneath the t-shirt with his busy, talented fingers, groaning when he found her bare flesh there.

He cupped her ass and lifted her up. Then, he whirled her around and set her on the cold, marble island. She started. "Does the marble turn you on or something?"

"What?" he laughed. "Any surface where I can lay your body out and devour it is a turn on."

"I remember." They both stilled, looking at each other for a long beat. Deciding whether they wanted to bring up the past from the ground where it lay dead and buried. Where it belonged. But with them, past was present, and present was prologue.

"I'm sorry." There he was, looking somber again.

She contemplated laughing it off. "For what?"

"For not being what you needed."

Shaking her head, she said, "You're what I need right now, for the next—" She looked out the window at the still falling snow. "For the next few days at least."

"Still, I would never hurt you, if I could at all prevent it."

He sure had a funny way of going about never seeing her get hurt—a threesome with his best friend and his ex was mighty complicated. She fully expected that she would leave this weekend with bruises—both the fun sex kind and the kind that affected her heart. The ones that may not heal up if she sustained them again.

"What about Lucas?" Frankie wasn't entirely sure that Lucas didn't have the same hopes for his relationship with Cary as she'd had a year ago. And, she didn't want him hurt either. Though he had a tough exterior, she had the feeling he reserved all of his softness for Cary. And he'd given her some of it holding her through the night.

"We're just friends who fuck sometimes." Cary shook his head. "And this weekend was sort of a last hurrah before we went into business together."

"No sticking your wick in the payroll?" She raised one brow, hoping to turn this back into a fun romp.

He rubbed his still hard cock against her open, wet center. If she looked down, there would likely be a wet spot on the front placard of his pants. She was a sick, twisted fuck to be so turned on by marking her territory on the front of his Christmas jammies.

"Not the payroll." He snaked his hand up the t-shirt and plucked at her nipple until she started. "We're partners, but we need clear boundaries."

"I'm not imposing?"

He bit his bottom lip and gave her nipple a harder pinch that made her moan. She should probably insist that they have this conversation while they were both fully clothed and didn't have their hands all over each other, but she didn't care to have him stop. It was the only thing keeping her from falling into despair about being stuck in D.C. for the holiday.

"If anything, it's less awkward having you here."

And then it dawned on her, and almost threw her off the lazy, meandering path to orgasm that he had her on. "You've done this before? Shared?"

"Not like this." He kissed the corner of her mouth, nipping a path along her jaw to her earlobe, all the while snaking his other hand up the t-shirt and rolling her other nipple between his fingertips. "Not for more than a few hours and not with anyone who—means something —to me."

She made the conscious decision to ignore the fact that he'd just admitted to having feelings for her. Or, rather, her vagina made that conscious decision. Her brain really didn't have anything to do with it. He didn't say anything else; he just kept driving her insane with his mouth and his hands until her hips rolled.

"You want me to fuck you, love?"

Then he pulled back, giving her a look that made her tingle from her toes to her clit.

"Yes, please." Then, he revealed that this had been in his plan all along by pulling a condom out of his pocket. "You planned this?"

"I had a feeling that you might box my ears and then need to work off your ire on my cock."

She laughed until he pulled down his pants, letting them pool on the floor. "Shirt off, love. I want to see your pretty tits bounce while a fuck you."

He was deadly filthy, and she freaking loved it. Couldn't get enough of him calling her "love" and telling her what he would do to her with his big cock. It got her almost as hot as the things he'd subsequently do.

In the past year, she'd tried to limit how often she thought of him. As their time apart had gone on, it had gotten easier because he wasn't implanting new filthy remembrances with each passing day. She whipped off the t-shirt, baring herself to him completely as she thought about how she'd never even be able to get a little turned on without thinking about him ever again. A twinge in her clit would be a memory of Cary putting a condom on and lining his dick up with her entrance before sliding inside her so hard her head tipped back.

"That's it, love." His posh accent gave way to a feral groan. "This island is really the perfect height to fuck you. I'll have to let my designer know he did a good job."

"He probably knew what you'd use it for." He withdrew a little, making her mewl, before setting a staccato pace that made her wish she could see the muscles of his ass moving. Maybe she'd get the chance to see him fuck Lucas before the holiday was over. It surprised her how much she wanted that. She'd always been such a jealous, territorial lover—with Lucas and Cary that didn't seem to apply. She wanted both of them too much for jealousy to come into play.

"Such cheek while my cock is inside of you." A few more strokes that singed every nerve ending below her waist. "Do you still do yoga?" She nodded, not knowing why he was asking about her fitness regimen while balls deep inside her. He revealed his motivation when he let go of her hips and grabbed her feet, placing them next to her on the counter, so she was in a deep squat.

It probably wasn't the most flattering position, but she couldn't seem to care when he thrust even deeper inside her. He had to hold her up so she wouldn't tip back and crack her head on the cold marble. Jesus, she was willing to risk her life to have this man deeper inside her.

"Rub your clit, love." His voice held the tone of an order, but she couldn't comply. If she let go of him, she'd fall. So, she shook her head. "I've got you. Let go and rub your clit so you come all over me. When I eat your pussy for breakfast, I want it after my cock takes you there."

That and a squeeze of his hands on her waist were all

she needed. She let go of one of his shoulders and found her clit. Her whole body seized because it was all too much, but he didn't let her fall.

In moments, she met his rhythm, feeling the thatch of hair at the base of his cock every time he pistoned inside her. She couldn't help herself, so she looked down and saw where they were joined. The sight of his covered cock wet and slick with her, his skin flushed and her accepting him while her fingers moved pushed her over.

As she contracted around him, he said, "That's it, love. Squeeze it. Give it all to me." Before her orgasm ended, his rhythm faltered, and he came inside her.

"So, good." But then again, it always was.

9

Even though he'd been desperate for caffeine and food, Lucas had stayed in bed while Francesca and Cary argued and then fucked downstairs. While the sight of them rutting together with all that raw elemental chemistry between them was immensely appealing, he wasn't emotionally tone deaf enough not to know that they had things they needed to sort out if they were going to have a weekend of decadence and filth all together.

He could have lied to himself and insisted that he only wanted Francesca to stay safe in the blizzard, but he was enough of a man to admit that he wanted her between him and his friend. She was beautiful and funny, and he was completely enchanted with her raw sensuality. The fact that he could see how much his friend wanted her only made her more appealing.

If he and Cary could only have one more weekend of whatever it was between them—him being in love with Cary, and Cary wanting to fuck him—then he wanted Francesca there as well. She was like a spark to their powder keg, and he didn't have the instinct for self-preservation not to want to explode before he walked away for good.

Despite the considerable self-control he'd displayed by not intruding on their row, he was more than half-hard when they came up the stairs laughing. Francesca stopped short at the door and stared at him. He put his hands behind his head, wanting to preen for her as her gaze raked all over his body. She bit her lip when her eyes hit his lap.

Cary came in behind her, and wrapped his arms around her waist, taking his time to appreciate Lucas' form under the sheet.

They both looked well-fucked if not sated. He couldn't miss the way that Cary touched her being different. His fingers dipped into her fleshy hips so firmly that he might leave bruises. It made Lucas want to tell him to ease up, even though his friend's feelings for her were not any of his business beyond this weekend.

"We've decided that we're all going to fuck until I can leave," said Francesca. "If that's okay with you?"

"More than okay." His tipped his head to his lap. "But it seems as though I'm behind in the count."

They both moved toward the bed, and Francesca crawled over to him, putting her mouth against his. Her swollen lips and playful tongue made him squirm. Even more, Cary stripping the duvet and sheet off his lap flayed him open for them.

They were really going to do this. Last night had opened up his brain and heart and rearranged things. He didn't know if anything would ever feel as right as being with Francesca with Cary in the room.

This, all of them touching—fucking—would be revolutionary. He didn't know if he would survive it.

Francesca pulled back and licked her bottom lip. She sat

back on her knees as though waiting for instructions. Cary didn't wait; he licked the bottom of Lucas' cock and sucked him down whole while Francesca just waited, juicy nipples pointing at him.

He didn't have the will to lick and suck and work her up with the way that Cary was set on making him come. It would only do to have her riding his face. He grabbed her waist.

"Up on my face, love"

She looked longingly at Cary's attentions on his cock. "But—"

"Face him if you must." He didn't blame her for not wanting to miss the show, and she complied. He only had a moment to admire all the pretty pink open for him, smell how turned on she was. Pure sex, this woman.

And it could have been a minute or maybe an hour before she bucked and smeared her honey all over his face as he came down Cary's throat. He didn't know; it was as though they were all suspended in time, like a lewd holiday snow globe as they fell away from each other panting on the bed.

Cary spoke first. "Best breakfast I've ever had."

Lucas agreed. He would wake up to it every day if he could ever get Cary and Francesca to agree that it was what they all needed.

It was strange having two people in his house when he wasn't throwing a cocktail party. Cary had renovated the place to entertain, but he'd never contemplated having a family holiday there. His parents had resigned themselves to one visit every year in the spring years ago, but they would never come to the States to spend a holiday in D.C.

They considered the whole nation to be tragically gauche, even nearly two and half centuries into its independence. And, merely by virtue of the fact that he had a real job, they considered him gauche as well. Although they never signaled their displeasure—another thing they considered positively plebian—it was evident in the way his mother sniffed and how her mouth formed around the word "profession."

If they had their druthers, he would have married one of the homely daughters of a noble family that they hadn't intermarried with for at least a century. He and his wife would have settled into a nearly sexless marriage, waltzing between an ancestral country home and a townhouse in town. The twenty-first century, nightmarish version of *Downton Abbey*.

But they'd made a grave mistake sending him off to boarding school where he'd been corrupted by news ideas like ambition, interclass marriage, and—partially through Lucas—pleasure. After university, there had been no going back, and his parents seemed to accept if not embrace that.

So, while he had a not-quite-cozy armistice going with his family, he'd never really expected to have a warm holiday season filled with laughter.

But, just like she had the year before, Francesca had taken him by surprise. He and Lucas had planned to ignore the holiday in favor of fine whisky and sex. Francesca refused to hear of it.

After breakfast, she'd looked them both in the eye, deadly serious, and said, "Why aren't there any decorations up?"

They hadn't had a good answer. "Aren't we decoration enough, love?"

"I think those nipple clamps Cary has would be a good stand-in for tinsel if you need sparkle." It warmed Cary to his bones that his friend was making jokes with Francesca when he so rarely displayed his humor for anyone but him.

Francesca stuck up a finger. "Put a pin in that, but I am talking about a tree and ornaments." She stood up and started pacing, looking only a tiny bit ridiculous in one of his soft cashmere sweaters and a pair of his pajama pants, her feet all cozy in a pair of too-large pair of woolen socks.

She looked like a present, but he had the feeling that he wasn't going to be able to unwrap her until there was some festive décor. He pondered whether he wanted to let her keep pacing and dressing him down for his festive failures or put her out of her misery right away. He exchanged a humorous glance with Lucas that made him want to string her along for a bit. He was enjoying this far too much in a life that hadn't held very much enjoyment.

It felt good to have him here, where he could see him every day and know that he was safe. He hadn't known that he'd needed that until he had it. Cary's chest filled with something that he'd label as tenderness if he didn't know any better.

Then Francesca stopped in her tracks. "You have decorations up in the attic from that Christmas in July fundraiser thingy you had here a few years ago."

Clever girl. Cary smiled and shrugged. "I'm sure we can cobble things together."

10

———————

Frankie struggled not to let herself get used to being around Cary and Lucas. Despite the fact that they were all going to be fucking each other's brains out in hours if not minutes, it felt very normal for Lucas to build a fire in the stone fireplace, and Cary to station her in front of it with a giant glass of wine and a bowl of popcorn with truffle shavings and real butter.

It felt truly lovely to have them give her a pointed look when she'd offered to help them put up the artificial—but very real looking—tree next to the fire. The fact that they didn't her to tell them how and where to place lights and ornaments was deeply satisfying in that it was such a break from her real life.

Now that she'd had eighteen hours to let her break-up with Ted settle in, her dominant emotion about the whole thing was relief. She was free, and she didn't have to worry about whether that man would say the wrong thing ever again. And, for her trouble, she had two men attending to her every whim—in and out of bed—for a long weekend.

Although she trusted Cary not to lie to her about the

weather, she'd checked in on the current report while he and Lucas hauled decorations down from the attic. Sure enough, she was likely to be stuck in D.C. for the next few days. She might be able to return to her condo the next day, but she didn't want to. As she watched Cary and Lucas do physical things, every so often rubbing up against each other when it wasn't strictly necessary, she wanted to stay here in this bubble with them forever.

She shook her head and took a sip of the very fine Bordeaux Cary had pulled out of his cellar for her "afternoon constitution." She would not get used to this. Cary had ended their relationship for a good reason—they didn't want the same things. Lucas and Cary were not going to continue fucking each other after the year turned—because they wanted to keep things professional.

Watching them together, it made her feel deeply sad. They fit together, and she'd never seen Cary as easy with anyone, including herself. Part of what made their relationship so compelling was that they barely agreed on anything. Cary was comfortable with Lucas, and she wanted that for him. He might have a very jaded view of relationships, but he deserved to be with someone who made him feel good— and Lucas was clearly that.

She should just be grateful that she got to be with both of them for a few days. Stolen moments that she would remember in fifty years after all the pertinent parts had been put into retirement.

Cary slid onto the couch next to her, pulling her torso so that her back leaned against his side. He wrapped one arm around her front but didn't slide his hand underneath the sweater she'd borrowed as she expected. He did take a handful of popcorn to crunch on, followed by a sip of her wine.

"Get your own."

"It is my wine, and you'll share if your pretty pussy wants a break. I'd much rather be drinking from there."

She peered up at him. So filthy, but so fun. No pretense with him when it came to sex. Lucas finished putting the gold angel on top of the tree. After checking to see that she didn't list to one side, he sat on the couch with her feet on his lap. She nearly purred at having his strong hand wrapped around the arch of sock-clad foot.

It was all so cozy that she couldn't help but be lulled by their breathing, the way Lucas' fingers danced against the skin on her ankles, Cary's hand in her mussed hair, the lights dancing against their faces, and the fire warming her to the core.

AT SOME POINT, Cary must have taken her glass and bowl and put them on the coffee table. She woke up as dusk fell, cuddled against Cary's thigh. He had his head thrown back against the back of the couch. Lucas also slept, slouched down, but still with her ankles in his hold.

The fire had died down without any of them awake to add kindling, and she absently thought of getting up to stoke the flames. But she was far too cozy at the moment to make any moves towards *doing* anything.

This was dangerous—feeling at home with them—but she couldn't seem to care. Just a few days—hours really at this point.

She'd almost been lulled into sleep when her phone rattled against the coffee table. Both men startled awake, and she made an apologetic face to both of them when she saw her aunt's face pop up.

"Hello?" Instead of speaking, Aunt Jean choked and sobbed. Any remaining sleepiness from her nap dissolved immediately. "What is it?"

"Heart attack," was all she could make out from the next sentence.

"Slow down, Jean." Cary and Lucas both moved closer to her on the couch. She wanted to swat them both away because she didn't want the comfort of their bodies close to hers at the moment. It didn't make sense, but she felt as though she deserved to feel the cold sadness seeping from her heart into her bones at the moment. As her aunt explained that Grams had had a heart attack and died in her sleep the night before, guilt replaced any happiness she'd been feeling waking up in their laps.

While her grandmother had been dying, she'd been *sinning*. Instead of making herself respectable before the eyes of the God of her grandmother's religion, she'd been enjoying the height of decadence. Even though she'd been a recovering Catholic for longer than she'd been a practicing one, but idea that she hadn't been there when her grandmother left this Earth made her feel as though she'd done something wrong and should be punished for it.

It didn't make logical sense. She knew it didn't. But that still didn't prevent her from turning in on herself and blaming herself for not leaving early yesterday, before the snow. She could have just pretended that Ted was about to propose and given her grandmother a few more hours of happiness—before she died.

Cary and Lucas were both so uncharacteristically still, and she could feel their wheels turning. Cary wanted to jump in and fix things—anything to prevent her from having messy feelings all over his expensive furniture—but this couldn't be fixed. And, though she'd only known him for a day, Lucas wanted to protect her from her troubles. As much as she appreciated it. She didn't deserve it. She didn't deserve them.

She deserved to be alone in her probably cold condominium for Christmas. She deserved to eat a frozen meal by herself.

And she would do just that, even if she had to walk across the city.

11

Cary scrubbed his hands through his hair and paced the living room after Francesca went upstairs with nary a word. He'd gleaned that her grandmother had died, and he knew that she had a complicated relationship with the woman from what she'd said when they were together before.

Right now, he wanted to break something because her grandmother's death had ruined their holiday, which he knew was petty and heartless. Most people had close relationships with their family. If he weren't a total ass, he would have found a way to comfort her. If he weren't such a selfish man, he would have found a way to get her home for the holiday after she'd been so distressed this morning.

Lucas sat on the couch, at the ready. "Should you go up there?"

Walking into the lion's den wasn't his usual strategy. He liked to skirt the edges while the lion bait was devoured before going in for the kill. Knowing her, she'd probably blame them for her grandmother dying in the first place, so he was the lion bait in this situation.

"She'll probably box my ears."

Lucas sat back on the couch. "She was bound to do that before the weekend ended regardless."

Cary stopped in his tracks and stared at his friend. "What are you talking about?"

"The two of you are a volatile combination, ready to explode at any second."

"That's why we broke up in the first place." Cary sat down in the arm chair, probably more dramatically than necessary. "We rub each other the right way until we rub each other the wrong way and have to go our separate ways."

Lucas shook his head as though Cary had just said something very stupid. "You don't feel it at all?"

"Feel what?" Cary grew more exasperated with each passing moment. Lucas was tossing out riddles at him when they needed to be figuring out how to fix this. "You're not making sense."

"You don't feel how good it was last night, earlier today?" Hurt tinged his friend's voice, which caught his attention. He looked at Lucas and saw something that he hadn't wanted to see before. Tenderness, love that would have come through if he hadn't just been focused on the lust. That was what having them both gave him.

Well of course he'd felt how good it was last night and earlier today. He usually felt pretty great with a mouth around his cock. But that didn't mean that this weekend was anything more than it actually was. A series of dirty interludes with two people he shouldn't be with but who turned him on.

If he kept them, he would be selfish. And he would hurt them just as his parents have hurt each other for decades.

"I think you've been blinded by too much pleasure at

once."

"You know, I'm not stupid. I see the way you look at her, and the way she looks at you. I feel the way she touches me. It's not how things are with the other girls I've seen you with. The other girls we've been with together."

He was right. Francesca was singular among women for him. She had been since he'd first spotted her at a cocktail party. It had taken him months in her social circle before he'd dared make an approach. His associates—he only counted Lucas among his real friends—had warned against her. Apparently, she had a reputation as quite the ball buster. But the more people warned him to stay away, the more he was drawn to her.

And it hadn't been good for either of them in the end. He should never have invited her here. It would have been better for everyone—including Lucas, who was looking more lovestruck by Francesca by the moment—if he had bought her a glass of wine and put her in a separate car last night.

He wouldn't feel flayed open and uncertain right now. "There's nothing I can do to fix this."

"You can't fix everything."

"I hate the woman for dying." It was the sort of thing he could only admit to someone he'd known for years. But he knew that Lucas had a fraught relationship with his family and would understand. "I just wanted—time with her."

"Her grandmother isn't my favorite either." Lucas sighed. "We should talk to her."

"I don't understand things like families." Cary's family barely fit the dictionary definition of the word with how much they all hated each other. "Perhaps we should just leave her alone."

Cary stood to go into the kitchen. Maybe he'd just bring

her a cup of tea. Lucas followed and hemmed him in against the counter. "You understand family better than you think." Cary stilled at the serious tone in Lucas' voice. "After all, you've been my family for years."

He turned and wished he hadn't. He didn't know if he could handle the earnest look on his friend's face. It made him want to reach for him in the way he'd never allowed himself to reach for Lucas. He'd always had the sneaking suspicion that Lucas had real feelings that went beyond sex, but he'd always pushed it away. He'd kept Lucas close, but never truly let him in. Letting him in would mean hurting him eventually. And he couldn't stand doing that.

This was why he didn't do feelings. They made him feel heavy and tethered the ground. They closed his throat and made him wonder if he was lonely instead of free.

Lucas surprised him by kissing his forehead. "Let's go talk to her."

FRANKIE HADN'T DARED hope that Cary and Lucas would follow her upstairs and try to comfort her. That wasn't what this was about. While she and Cary had been dating, he one time she'd started crying over something shitty that one of her coworkers had done, he hadn't hugged her or soothed her. He went ahead and fixed it. Thinking of it now, she should have cut her losses at that point. That way, she wouldn't have been hurt when he'd stated the obvious and told her he couldn't commit to her.

If he couldn't handle her at a hot mess, he didn't deserve her at her hard ass bitch.

She'd gone upstairs to lay on a bed in one of the guest rooms to be alone with her feelings. Maybe it made her an asshole, but she felt relieved. As though her shoulders had one less thing to carry. She'd been preparing for her grandmother's eventual death for months and had dreaded getting reports from her family about her slowly disappearing from herself. Her grandmother was sharp and vain, and she would have hated fading away.

Her grandmother had presence that would have been snuffed out by dementia, and it would have been painful to watch her die. It was painful to lose a woman who had loved her—if only conditionally. Frankie's parents had been totally accepting of everything she wanted to do and be in life, but her grandmother had been exacting. There had been a kinship between her and her grandmother, which was why she'd always wanted to please her more than anything.

Now that she was gone, she didn't have to please anyone but herself. Mixed in with the relief she felt that her grandmother wouldn't suffer, she felt a freedom she hadn't in a long time.

All her tears were dry, and she was smiling when Cary and Lucas walked into the room with gentle looks on their faces and caution in their steps.

"Are you okay?" Lucas asked first, which surprised her. It shouldn't. Though he looked like he could smash a head like a rotten melon between his meaty paws, he was definitely the soft touch when it came to the two of them. With her newfound freedom, she felt free to wanting to keep his soft touch.

"My grandmother's dead."

"And you're smiling?" Cary, ever the logician, needed to point that out.

She patted two spots on the king bed, on either side of her. This wasn't what they were here for—emotions and family drama were for therapy, not dirty weekends—but they'd opened the door by coming up here.

They sat down and didn't run downstairs to see how fast they could have her committed, so that was good.

"She had dementia." She took a deep breath. "And it was rapidly progressing, so this weekend would have been my last chance to see her when she was—still her."

Lucas put a steadying hand on her knee—calm, steady. Before this weekend, she'd never thought that she would have feelings as intense as she'd had for Cary. Astonishingly, Lucas made her feel the same way. He drew her in as much as Cary. It warmed her all over, and she leaned her head on his shoulder even though it was probably just too much. But she wanted the comfort of his body, and she wasn't in the mood to deny herself. Life was too short.

Cary still hung back. "I'm so sorry for your loss." Of course, he knew the right sounds to make, but there was no emotion behind the words.

"My family—my grandmother had a strange way of showing she loved me." Lucas turned her hand and strung her fingers between his. "The last time we talked before the diagnosis, she basically told me that all my accomplishments were worthless if I didn't get married and have a family."

Cary's body jerked as though she'd slapped him across the face. "So, when you wanted more of a commitment from me?"

Frankie shook her head. "That was about you and me." She reached out to touch him even though she was afraid it might drive him away. He surprised her by taking her other hand and kissing the palm. "Ted was about my grand-mother. If he would have cooperated, we could have had a nice life together, but it wasn't what I wanted."

All along, she'd wanted Ted to be Cary. All along, she'd known that was a dumb wish to have because Cary was indelible. He was one-of-a-kind, and she'd never meet anyone who held a candle to him. Yes, Ted had been about giving up. Ted had been settling. She was relieved that she didn't have to settle.

And that was before she'd known Lucas and how much she could feel for the two men sitting on the bed with her. She'd wanted Ted to be Cary, but she needed to be with Cary and Lucas. Right now, and maybe forever.

Cary kept her hand, but he looked down. "I'm sorry I wasn't there for you. I couldn't be what you needed."

Frankie didn't know what to say, but Lucas scoffed. "You're such an idiot." She snorted because *no one* talked to Cary like that if they liked to stay living and working in D.C. Talking back to him was less risky for her because he liked how she sucked his cock. But she rather liked that Lucas could get away with it effortlessly. The two of them together might just be able to keep his ego in check. "You think you're bad at being in relationships when we've been in a relationship of sorts for years."

"But we're friends—"

"And we very much enjoy fucking each other."

"But we both date other people."

"Not lately."

Silence fell for a beat until Cary tried to wheel everything back. "Francesca was with Ted."

That made Frankie want to apologize, but she stopped herself. Cary broke up with her, and she'd moved on. Nothing to feel guilty about. She was however interested in what Cary didn't say. He didn't point out the number of women he'd been out with in the year since they'd broken up. "That's ridiculous. Cary is out with a different congressional aide every week."

Lucas met her gaze, look of concern gone, cheeky grin firmly back in place. "But you forget that he doesn't mix business with pleasure."

Frankie looked back at Cary. He said, "He's right."

"So, no one?" It should not turn her on that he hadn't been with another woman since her. She was supposed to be sex-positive and progressive, but a primal part of her brain would always look at Cary and scream, "Mine!"

That he'd been with Lucas should bother her as much as him being with another woman, but the screaming, feral fuck monster they'd awoken in her had also claimed him. Cary felt like hers; Lucas as well. And, sitting there in the moment, she felt like—theirs.

If only she could convince Cary that he was already good at relationships. He cared more than he wanted to admit. He might not soothe, but he fixed things. And, in that moment, she realized that he hadn't dumped her because he just wasn't that into her. He'd broken things off because she'd gotten too close. And, really, she hadn't gotten any further away in the year since they'd broken up.

He hadn't been with anyone else.

But he still didn't know that they were all in love with each other. Cary had been in love with Lucas for years. She was in love with Cary. And she'd fallen for Lucas practically at first sight—probably because of how much he loved Cary.

It just wasn't clear whether he would let them in. The only thing she did know was that she needed to touch both of them now. Needed to show them how she felt about them.

So, she crawled into Cary's lap, wrapped her arms around his neck, and kissed him.

12

———————

Cary caught Francesca up in his arms, needing to feel her against him. He hadn't slept with another woman since they'd broken up because—along with Lucas—she was his home, and no amount of denying it would change that simple fact. They hadn't dated for very long, but already she felt as familiar to him as Lucas. Her lips against his were a soothing balm, and her scent in his nostrils made him feel young again.

If she kept shifting her hips, rubbing against his cock, he was going to come right away, and this would all be over much too fast. So, he set her away from him, and looked over at Lucas. He didn't want either of them to think that this wasn't about the three of them—together. He was gratified that there was no hesitation when he said, "Kiss her."

While Lucas devoured her mouth and kept Francesca's hands busy with the buttons of his shirt, Cary removed her pants and maneuvered her out of his sweater—very convenient attire for getting her naked.

Her mouth was swollen and red when she looked back

at him, and he couldn't resist biting her fat lower lip. She truly was criminally beautiful, and she belonged to them whether she was ready to admit that or not.

"Why are you the only one still fully clothed?" she asked as she reached for the button on Lucas' pants. "He's much more cooperative than you are."

"It's always been that way, love." Lucas said, unzipping and kicking away his pants so that Cary was the only one in an unfortunate state of having clothes on. "He was always getting in trouble, and I was always the teacher's pet."

Cary didn't respond but stripped as both his lovers watched. He liked having both of them looking at him as though they couldn't wait for what came next. He liked seeing their hands roving each other's bodies. He never would have thought he could watch anyone else touching Francesca; he'd wanted to crush her ex-almost-fiancé's head between his palms when he'd seen them at that restaurant the night before. With Lucas it was different—they both belonged to him.

He crawled over the bed to them and kissed them each on the mouth, taking in how Francesca moaned when he and Lucas kissed inches from her face. "You like watching us?"

"You're not the only one who likes watching, Sir Cary." He liked her calling him "sir," even though he wasn't into formalities in the bedroom. Maybe they'd explore that later, much later.

"How about you watch me fuck him while he eats your pussy?" Her eyes widened, as though he'd offered her a plate of her favorite Christmas biscuits. Then, he looked to Lucas, who bit his bottom lip and nodded. "You'll eat her pussy and rub your cock. And I'll make you both come."

"If you say so...Sir Cary." Lucas's tone was insolent, but he was already following the second part of his instruction.

Cary went into the hall bathroom and found condoms—a whole strip of them—and a bottle of lube. He didn't plan to leave the bedroom for the rest of the holiday for anything but food, and he had no intention of under-provisioning himself. At times, his tactical ability was a curse. This wasn't one of them.

When he returned to the bedroom, Lucas was sucking on Francesca's nipples, and her fingers were buried in his thick black hair. Cary rubbed his hand over Lucas' spine, and felt him shudder from the touch. Although they'd been fooling around alone and with others for years, they hadn't done this in a while. And sex with Lucas had never been quite as meaningful. As much as he was claiming Francesca —with no plans for letting her go—he was claiming Lucas as well.

When Francesca had climbed on his lap and wrapped her arms around him, a dam broke inside him. The way she looked at him as though he was enough for her, the way she clung to him even though he'd hurt her. And the way that Lucas understood him more deeply than anyone else in his life. They both trusted him. They both fit him. And he would do anything to keep them both.

Including feelings.

The look on Francesca's face as she narrated what Cary was doing—putting on a condom, slathering lube everywhere, fondling Lucas' cock, opening up his asshole with his fingers—was a gift that no one else could give him. But her legs shifted restlessly on the bed, and she needed Lucas's mouth on her pussy. So, he slapped Lucas' flank lightly. "Get on with it, mate."

Lucas gave him a scathing look that had no heat behind it but told him that there would be payback. Payback that Cary very much looked forward too. When Lucas got his mouth on her and Cary lined up his cock at Lucas' entrance, Francesca flexed her hands in the air as though she wasn't sure what to do with them, as though the sensory inputs were too much.

He paused. "Are we doing this?" He would stop right now if she wasn't okay with this, if she'd asked for everything but found she wanted to stop here. And although everything had changed with Lucas and they would be mixing business with pleasure on an almost hourly basis. Just as he'd figure out a way to let her go if she didn't want to be with them after this weekend. It would be painful, both his heart and his cock would be sad and battered, but he would do it.

"Yes," she moaned. "I just don't know what to do with my hands."

He smiled at her, relieved that she was still on board. "Put them above your head, through the slats on the headboard. You can remove them when I fuck you because I like the way you try to pull my hair out while I'm deep inside you."

After he spoke, he worked himself inside Lucas' tight hole. Lucas pushed back until he was fully inside him, and Cary had to stop. He squeezed his eyes closed and wished he could plug his ears for a moment, so he didn't come right away. He wanted this to last, but the conflagration of how right this felt was set to take his whole body—and it was tempting to let it.

But he felt and equal and opposite need to draw out the pleasure. He opened his eyes to a feast in front of him, more tempting than anything that would cover a Christmas Eve dinner table. Lucas' strong back arched and his head bowed in worship between Francesca's thighs. Her naked body spread out in a lurid display. It was decadent, some would say sinful, but to Cary it felt like home.

He was hitting the right spot if the muffled curses coming from Lucas' mouth were any indication. Cary barely kept a tether on his own orgasm as Lucas jerked and spilled all over the coverlet.

Cary pulled out and grabbed a new condom as Lucas continued eating Francesca's pussy. He wouldn't relieve him from his efforts until she'd come. He planned to keep the precious girl so sated with orgasms that she wouldn't have the strength to leave when the holiday ended. If he played his cards right, she would stay with them forever.

In moments, her whole body shuddered with pleasure, and she cried out. Her back came off the bed, and her neck arched up so pretty that Cary had to kiss the moans right out of her mouth.

When he pulled back and she opened her eyes, she looked down at the rather severe hard-on he still sported. She was like the answer to a prayer when she said, "Fuck me."

Lucas pulled away from her, his mouth slick with her come, and Cary pulled his head towards his to taste both of his lovers at once. Heaven.

When he pulled back, Lucas lounged against the headboard, next to Francesca, hard again. He gave her a kiss as Cary pushed inside her swollen gate. As he'd instructed, Francesca drove her fingers into his hair even as Lucas appeared to be driving her mad with his fingers on her clit.

It was the brush of Lucas's fingers against her clit as Cary drove inside her over and over again that finally did it. Francesca's pussy contracting around him, his vision went blurry at the edges as he came and came inside her before falling into a sweaty pile with both of them.

Perfect.

13

———

Frankie hated that they'd eventually had to leave the spare bedroom for food. But as a public relations professional, she couldn't say that *Throuple Dies on Christmas Because They Were Too Horny to Feed Themselves* was a good look.

So, eventually, she'd let Cary and Lucas make her dinner. Just steak, brussels sprouts, and mashed potatoes, but it felt like a total luxury to watch them moving around the kitchen together. It was all so domestic at the same time, and she found herself thinking that she could get used to the three of them living like this.

A very dangerous thought because neither of them had explicitly said that they wanted to be with her after this interlude—much less the both of them. And she'd learned her lesson about assuming that a man wanted to be with her permanently almost a day ago now.

After dinner, they'd had more sex. This time, Lucas had fucked Cary's face with such vigor that she'd actually been concerned for that little dangly thing at the back of Cary's throat. But then, Cary had winked at her as Lucas had come, as if to warn her that she was in for it as soon as Lucas was finished with him. After that, it was all a delicious blur.

Given how many orgasms she'd had in the last twenty-four hours, she shouldn't have had any problems sleeping. But when she woke up with only one side of her body blanketed in Cary's manly warmth, her bladder and her curiosity about Lucas' whereabouts prevented her from falling back to sleep.

She grabbed another one of Cary's cashmere sweaters and a pair of shorts from his drawer, wishing she could pilfer half his wardrobe before she left. All of his clothes were perfectly fitted to his body, but she swam in them and it felt lovely. She didn't mind the way his scent lingered in the fine fibers either.

Once she used the bathroom, she heard movements from the kitchen. She padded down the cold stairs and found Lucas in the kitchen rolling out what looked like dough.

"What are you doing?" He didn't start from her sudden appearance, so he must have known she was there.

"It was supposed to be a surprise." He sounded vaguely disappointed, and it was so adorable she wanted to ruffle his already mussed hair. Her heart throbbed with love for him, and she wondered at how that was even possible.

"I'm surprised you—former super-spy—gets up in the middle of the night and bakes." She was surprised and mesmerized by the way his forearms flexed as he worked a rolling pin. No wonder she'd noticed bruises where he'd held her thighs open for Cary a few hours ago—he trained them.

"My father was a baker." He paused and patted the corner on the other side of the sink. She hopped up, hopeful that he'd share more if she sat with him. It astonished her how little she knew about this man who had taken her body to previously unknown heights and somehow pitched a tent in her heart in less than a day. "Before he found a way to send me to Eton, I used to get up and help him before school."

"And now you can't sleep late?" It was about four in the morning, hours until it would be light outside, but every muscle in Lucas' body was already alert.

"Never could get used to the decadence of sleeping until seven."

She laughed at his wry humor. "What are you making?"

"Croissants." He couldn't have made her happier if—no, he couldn't have made her happier, full stop.

"Are you a cyborg designed purely for my pleasure? Between the sex and croissants, I'm beginning to believe you aren't real." That earned her one of his rare laughs. "Is your father still alive?"

His smile disappeared, and she got the sneaking suspicion she'd said the wrong thing. Maybe not as wrong as assuming that Ted would propose but wrong all the same. The last thing she wanted to do when Lucas had been so great about taking her mind off things this weekend. "I'm sorry. I shouldn't have said anything."

"It's alright." He paused in rolling out dough and looked at her. From the moment he'd set his gaze on her at the restaurant the other night, she'd felt pinned whenever he'd put the intensity of his full attention on her. Like an insect specimen in the museum. So, she didn't move, just waited for him to speak again. "He was a bit of a drunk, but still a good dad. I loved him a lot. He loved me, but he didn't really understand why I didn't want to stay in our little village and get up at 4:30 every morning and bake bread for the same people I grew up with until I dropped dead of a heart attack at 75."

That was the most he'd ever said—she had the feeling—maybe ever. "I loved my Gran, too."

"Of course you did." He went back to his task, wrapping the laminated dough in plastic and walking it over to the fridge. "You wouldn't have tried to marry a fool if you hadn't loved your grandmother."

"Ted's not a fool." She looked down and traced the metallic glints in the marble with one finger. "He was right not to want to commit to me. I didn't love him."

Lucas was in front of her then. "You were always in love with Cary."

She wanted to deny it, but a part of her had longed for Cary since the first time they'd met. She wanted to deny it now because it was clear that Lucas loved him, too. She hoped that Lucas loved her as much as she was coming to love him. And she wasn't foolish enough to think that all three of them could make a go of things together. They lived in a city where people lived and died by their reputations. Nothing could be more reputation busting than living in a permanent ménage.

Cary's job was to make sure that rumors stayed rumors. The truth of them together would be far too scandalous for all of them.

"You're in love with him, too." She looked down again, not wanting to be confrontational. It wasn't an accusation; it was as truthful as the sun coming up in the East and flirting with the edges of the horizon in that moment.

But he wouldn't let her escape. He wedged his big, delicious body in between her legs and lifted her chin with one finger. "I am."

She wished, more than anything, that everything she was feeling right now made sense to her. But it didn't. Falling in love with not one, but two men at first sight was a fantasy. It wasn't something that happened in real life. Especially so when the two men who also happened to have a complicated relationship history of their own. A holiday of mind-blowing sex didn't form the basis of a lasting relationship—or even a fleeting one. All the things she wanted with both of them were too much to ask of a universe that hadn't been terribly generous with her lately. Tears formed in her eyes—not the icy cold ones of sharp grief she'd cried earlier—but hot, wet tears. The kind that made her want to throw herself on the floor and scream until she got what she wanted.

"What are we going to do?" She let out an almost-hysterical laugh. "I'm not going to be jealous when he ends up with you."

"Of course, you won't be," he said it as though his determined tone could make it true. "You're going to be with both of us."

"We can't—"

He kissed her on the mouth, cutting off the rest of what she'd planned to say. All of her misgivings and rational reasons why they couldn't all be in love with each other flew out of her mind when his dry, hot lips moved over hers. He tasted of toothpaste and smelled like yeast and flour and sleep. She wanted to roll in the way he smelled and looked and felt under her hands as she gripped his shoulders and pulled him closer.

Lucas didn't come off as an idealist; he couldn't truly be a romantic given the things he'd done and seen in his previous profession. But she was willing to abide in his surety for the moment. They were still stuck inside from the storm, and she could live in her fantasy world for just a little while longer.

Giving him further permission, she pulled up his t-shirt. He stopped kissing her just enough to let her pull it off and relieve her of her sweater. Then, they were skin-to-skin in the room where all of this had started. She hoped they would have more moments upstairs in the giant master suite. In her fantasies, all three of them would explore just how dirty they could get in a steaming hot shower. But every moment that she had in this house with either or both of these men was stolen from her real life.

So, she let everything go, lifted her hips when he pulled off her shorts. Canted her hips up to meet his cock when he pushed his sweats down and put on the condom he'd conveniently brought down from the bedroom.

She threw her head back and laughed when he explained, "Knew someone would want to fuck me for making pastry." And she bit his shoulder so hard it would likely leave a mark when he fucked her hard to stop her laughing.

After that, they were silent and frantic. They're skin grew slick with sweat as he fucked into her as though he wanted to imprint himself on her body. When he reached down and rubbed her clit, she bucked against his hand. Combined with all the emotion of the moment, she couldn't hold out.

Lucas drove her mad, just by being himself. She wanted to wrap herself around him and never, ever let go. Wanted his steadfast heart in her hands and his big, hard body under her fingers all the time. But she didn't think she could have it. No one had it all. Even the people who looked like they did. Especially them.

It was almost sorrowful when she came, wishing that this wasn't one of the last times they'd do this together. But she didn't tear up when he whispered in her ear that he wanted to keep her forever as he was coming, when he collapsed on top of her briefly before gently redressing her.

She'd cry later when she was alone in her condo, wishing she was back here with them.

14

It was just as well that Francesca and Lucas had both vacated his bed by the time Cary woke up. He needed to go to his study to make plans, and he didn't want to fight off the temptation to stay in bed with them for the rest of the day.

Their tryst was going to come to an end. If he wanted to keep Lucas as his best friend and didn't want to gut Francesca eventually when he hurt her. He wanted it to last forever too much for his wish to come true. And, he knew that he would have a hard time convincing Lucas that they could work together while romantically entangled. And Francesca—she was willing become engaged to a total dipshit just to make her grandmother believe she'd found love. Anyone who cared that much about appearances wouldn't want to be in a relationship with two men.

He might have momentarily fooled himself the night before while they'd been tangled together in this bed, but he was too pragmatic in the cold light to dawn to keep that belief alive.

After all, her job was all about—as she'd once said—

"putting lipstick on some real pigs." It would be impossible to apply enough cosmetics to a permanent ménage-a-trois to satisfy her need to feel respectable.

She'd have questions that he couldn't provide the answer to—like what would they do about holidays where they weren't trapped in D.C. Though her grandmother had passed, she'd probably want to go home. And, soft heart that she was, she wasn't going to leave one or both of them behind to spend the holiday alone. Francesca loved very hard, but her loyalty often worked to her detriment even as it was one of the reasons she was simply incomparable.

And she'd probably worry about his business, though no one would dare look at him askance if they became public. He had so many secrets about the most powerful people in this town that anyone who said a word could be destroyed in three phone calls or less. And if things got really bad, he had a title and land in England. They could go there and not see anyone, save anyone but servants, for the rest of their lives.

After this weekend, she wouldn't be comfortable continuing a relationship with just Cary. Her connection with Lucas was just as obvious to him as how he felt about Lucas. And Cary didn't want just one of them either. In his mind, after last night, she and Lucas were a package deal. And he was sad that he couldn't puzzle his way around this and fix it.

He could fix everything.

Speaking of his power in this town, he had work to do. By the time he was done, fifteen minutes later, he was certain that this was the last time Francesca would look at him with her open, loving expression.

He went in the kitchen, ignoring his growling stomach at

the scent of rich pastry—Lucas was just as good with baking as he was with sucking cock. So, very very good.

Francesca's face lit up, and his stomach fell.

"You should put some warmer clothes on." That's all he could think to say? Her forehead wrinkled, and Lucas sat forward in his chair.

"Why? You keep it warm enough in here that I could wander around naked."

As much as he'd like that, he needed to end this now. He couldn't keep her here when she should be with her family. It wasn't right. "The roads are clear enough for a car—a truck—to pick you up in—" He checked his watch. "Fifteen minutes."

"You're sending me away?" She was confused, and he was mucking this up terribly.

He couldn't look at her when he said, "I've arranged for a private plane to take to you to Minneapolis."

"You're sending me away." He turned and walked over to the coffee maker. If he saw the tears that clogged her voice, he wouldn't be able to go through with this. It was for the best. This couldn't last, and she would regret not spending this time with her family.

"You need to say goodbye to your grandmother."

"And we're not even going to talk about what happens next?" There it was. Enough anger had seeped into her voice that he could stand looking at her.

"What happens next is that you go home in time to spend Boxing Day with your family." He paused to pour a cup of coffee. "And then you return to your life."

"We don't even celebrate Boxing Day, you fucking idiot."

"That seems a little harsh for a man who just got you on a flight before the airports even opened back up—officially."

Francesca paced the floor of the kitchen; her small feet

making exaggerated slapping sounds against the tile. He liked her in his kitchen and in his bed—far too much. He'd let himself indulge too far in fantasies of having her here with him all the time. But he didn't live in the world of fantasy.

"I just can't believe your ending this—" She motioned towards Lucas, herself, and him. "Without any discussion."

"Believe it." Disdain dripped from Lucas' words. He can't have expected Cary to handle things any differently? This was the only logical conclusion of their affair. Ended amicably.

Francesca stared at him with her hands on her hips for a long moment before she turned and left the room. Over her shoulder she said, "I'm stealing this sweater and a pair of your cozy pants!"

"The driver already picked up your clothes," he shot back. "But you're welcome."

That sounded lame, even to his ears.

As the car pulled out of the drive with the tearful but resolved Frankie safe inside, Lucas grabbed Cary's arm and wheeled him around. He was ready to box his ears. It was—by far—the dumbest thing he'd ever done. Dumber than the time he'd gotten arrested in Thailand because his ex couldn't go twenty-four hours without cocaine. Letting Francesca walk out the door without promises exchanged was stupid. He'd woken up that morning, before daylight, knowing in his bones that he was where he belonged. And now Cary had mucked things up by making a rash decision that they couldn't make things work.

But the difference was —unlike the time in Phuket—it

affected his life. Lucas wanted to be with Francesca and Cary, and he needed to convince Cary that all three of them could make a go of it. He may be a man of few words, but he would take action as soon as he knew what he wanted. He wanted them to be an *us*.

Cary looked down at Lucas' hand on his arm. "I'm not really in the mood after that display, mate."

"I'm not trying to fuck you." Lucas let his arm go and stepped back. "I'm more tempted to shake some sense into your dumb arse."

"Not even a little impressed that I managed to summon a private plane out of thin air?"

Lucas suppressed the need to growl. Cary would probably change his mind about being in the mood to fuck if he went full Hulk-smash. "I'm not impressed that you let the best thing that ever happened to us leave."

Cary shrugged, but looked down at his suddenly interesting feet. For one of the most powerful men in D.C., he sure had a way of behaving like a sullen child. "She would have left anyway."

"Maybe." Chances were, their relationship might not last forever. Maybe she'd decide that the two of them were too much, and she'd want to go back to dating assholes like Ted. But he doubted it. Cary always got what he wanted, and he'd always made sure that Lucas got what he wanted. If he wanted them to be with Francesca, that's what would happen. His lover removed obstacles with the force of his personality the way Lucas eliminated them with a more brutal form of force. "Do you not want her?"

Cary's head snapped up. "You bloody well know I do." He wrapped his arms around his body, grasping his elbows —a sure sign that he was falling apart. "But she would not— and you wouldn't. I'd fuck it up."

"Probably." Lucas admitted. Being in a relationship with two of the most stubborn people he'd ever met was not something he would do if he were overly concerned about being logical. But he hadn't decided to fall in love with his best friend. He'd come here to figure out how to say good-bye to the youthful adventures they'd had—to change their relationship to one that was strictly professional. But then fate had seen fit to add Francesca to the mix, and the chemical reaction between the three of them had shifted his objective. "But the idea of not trying—"

Lucas waited for the wheels to stop turning in Cary's head. He might be falling apart, but he would put himself together and find a way to fix this after he'd kicked himself enough.

"Not trying was stupid." Lucas wanted to kiss him, but there would be time for that once they'd retrieved Francesca from the airport. "You'd really want to be in a relationship? For me?"

The "and not just for Francesca" was unspoken. He and Cary had spent so long denying that they were in a relationship with each other—the longest and most enduring of both their lives. But Lucas was done denying it. He was in love with both of them, and he didn't care about the consequences from the outside world. The promise of having Francesca and Cary as his own was too tempting to let doubts get in the way.

Maybe he needed to build in some kissing and making up into the journey. He stepped towards Cary and put him close by the shoulders. Then, he kissed him—not anything meant to end in rolling around on the floor, but something to reassure his friend and lover.

But it turned into more. Lucas poured all of his love and tenderness into his kiss and waited for Cary to respond.

Only when Cary grabbed his face and pulled him close, trying to dominate, did Lucas pull back.

"I came here for you. It would have been torture to work with you every day after having been your lover for years."

Cary placed his hands on his chest. "Utter torture."

"What do you say we go get our girl?"

"I'll call another car."

By the time Francesca arrived at the airport, she was *seething*. She was, of course, angry at Cary. He'd tricked her into falling in love with him all over again. He'd dangled something that she'd fantasized about for years in front of her and then ripped it away when the fantasy became too real for him.

And Lucas? She'd expected him to do something. She knew that Cary could be implacable, but good God!

She was torn as to whether she wanted to let either of them get away with it. If they wanted her out of their lives, they would get it. And then she'd go about taunting them by being seen with every man in town he hated until they broke. Because they weren't done with her or their unconventional relationship. Cary hadn't even been able to look her in the eye as he'd practically ordered her out of his house.

The nerve!

Even though she was incensed about Cary's asshole behavior and worried the Lucas might not be able to save it, it was difficult to be too angry on a private plane. Especially one with champagne and snacks that she didn't have to share with anyone. But part of her missed Lucas stealing cheese and fruit from her plate when he had plenty of his own. That's how she knew she was more than a little bit in love with him—she'd never willingly shared cheese with another man.

As she sat alone, waiting for the plane to taxi and take-off, doing her level-best to make small talk with the flight attendant, she realized that she would have liked Cary and Lucas to come with her. She didn't care if her parents thought she'd lost it by having an affair with two men. And she didn't care about what anyone else in D.C. thought about it either. It wasn't as though any of them would be cheating. And any person who liked dudes would probably give her a high-five for snagging two of the hottest men on the planet. Given the prevalence of adultery in Washington, their affair was almost quaint.

It wasn't conventional, but when had she ever been conventional? If she'd lived according to her grandmother's standards, she'd have been married for over a decade with many, many children. But she was ambivalent about motherhood, and she'd always felt like marriage would be too limiting. That was probably whey she'd chosen to be with Cary in the first place.

But Cary and Lucas had unlocked a desire for permanence she'd never had when it came to relationships. Before, she'd over-analyzed and been in her head half the time. With them, she just allowed herself to feel what she felt and say what she needed to say. She'd never have called Ted a "fucking idiot"—at least not to his face. But with Cary and Lucas, she wasn't afraid that they'd hold it against her. Especially since Cary was, in fact, behaving like a total idiot.

And Lucas had let her down. She'd expected him to

stand up and do something, make Cary see sense before it was too late. It might be too much to convince them both that being a *they* was worth a try.

She drained her glass of champagne—not exactly a mourning beverage, but she could never say no to champagne—and pressed the button for another before take-off. She'd like to be drunk for her grandmother's funeral.

To her surprise, the flight attendant didn't appear. Instead, a breathless and red-faced Cary walked into the cabin, followed by a somewhat smug-looking Lucas. He winked at her, and she fought the urge to smile at their arrival. They both had quite a bit of explaining to do before she forgave them.

Well, some explaining and kissing and making up. She wouldn't punish them for too long. It had only taken an hour for Cary to see sense.

"What are you doing here?" She tried to keep her voice sounding stern.

Cary sat in the chair next to her and buckled his seatbelt. The flight attendant appeared with three full glasses of champagne. Her eyebrows went up when she took in the full effect of Frankie's two men and then she disappeared.

"We're going with you," Cary said, as though he didn't have any fast talking to do.

"If that's okay?" Lucas at least phrased it like it was her option, so she grabbed his knee and squeezed.

"You're coming with me as what?" If Cary thought he could just show up and have that be the end of things, he had another think coming. As much as he abhorred them, they were going to have a relationship-defining conversation before he got to meet her parents and cousins.

Lucas snagged her attention. "Whatever you'll let us come with you as, love." She looked at him, shocked to realize that when he called her "love," he meant everything that went along with that word.

Still, she needed more. "I need to hear it from him."

Cary took a drink of champagne. "Your lovers."

"I'm not going to tell my parents that I'm having a fling with two men." For one thing, her father's head would explode. "If you're coming with me, we're in a relationship."

"You'll tell them you're with both of us?" Cary sounded surprised.

"I realized while I was in the car and while I was sitting alone on the plane you put me on *to send me away* that I didn't feel like I was going to see my family." She took Cary's hand. "I felt as though I'd just left my family."

"You've only known me a few days." Lucas said.

Frankie shrugged. "But you're mine, all the same."

"And you're ours." Cary unclipped his seatbelt and fell to his knees in front of her. "If you'll have us."

"I didn't drop kick you out of the airplen, so I guess I'll have you."

They had to take their seats for take-off, but once they were in the air and the captain thought it was safe to move around the cabin, Lucas and Cary pulled her into the best part of having a private plane—the bedroom.

The door latched, they were all naked in less than a minute. She didn't know how it happened so quickly because one of them always had his mouth on hers. As Cary kissed down the side of her neck, Lucas nibbled her mouth.

"This would have been a much better way to start the morning," Frankie said.

"Agreed." Lucas moved her hair off of her neck and kissed the spot at the back while Cary knelt at her feet for the second time that day.

"Spread your legs, love." Cary kissed her between her legs before she complied.

Behind her, she heard Lucas rip open a condom. "Hopeful that this would turn out your way, weren't you?"

"Lucas is ever the optimist," Cary said before he sucked her clit into his mouth.

It was so intense that she reflexively tried to move away. But she moved right to where Lucas was sheathed and ready for her. "Bend over, love."

Cary paused, and it filled her with panic. She grabbed at his rakishly disheveled hair and pulled him back towards her pussy. "Keep going."

"Your wish." She liked the sound of that. They'd already filled her every wish since Christmas Eve Eve.

Sex with two hot men? Check.

Love from said two hot men? Check.

Her grandmother's approval? Probably not, but why the fuck would she care when she had the first two?

Lucas lined his cock up at her entrance and pushed inside easily. He reached around her body and loosely cupped her throat, pulling her head back to kiss him on the mouth. Knowing how much she liked her nipples pinched, Cary reached up and pinched them hard enough that she would feel it after they were done.

Everything was sound and light and they were the only three people who ever existed, flying high above West Virginia. They were everything she'd never known she'd always wanted, and nothing else mattered.

When her orgasm started, she felt Lucas jerk and lose rhythm as he came inside her. She'd never ever tire of making him lose control and grunt his pleasure into her mouth. Cary stood and kissed them both before Frankie pushed him onto the bed.

"Condom?" Lucas asked, ever the tactician.

Frankie shook her head. "Want him in our mouths."

"How did I get so very lucky?" Cary asked as they crawled on the bed next to him.

"I don't think Santa Clause takes these kinds of requests." Frankie said.

Lucas and Cary both laughed. "Only from you, love," Cary said, pulling her up to his mouth for a kiss. "Now, my cock is hard, and I need Santa's helpers to take the edge off."

'Twas the night before Christmas, and Frankie's moans could be very faintly heard from all the way in Cary's study. Unfortunately, he was stuck on a conference call. Hearing Lucas make their lover sound possessed and not being able to participate wasn't the only reason that his patience with this interminable Zoom call was running thin, but it was the primary one.

Still a man of action, he stood up and closed the door, so he could unmute the call. He didn't even care that he cut the senator's chief of staff off when he said, "Gentlemen, we all have families and holidays to get to—"

"Cary George, family man." He didn't miss the derisive note coming from a lowly staffer. He lowered his glasses on his nose and glared at the young man who had probably heard salacious rumors about the fact that he was in a relationship with both his business partner and best friend and the best public relations flack in town.

Cary had destroyed careers and gathered and leaked evidence that had taken down politicians the media had deemed invincible. He'd covered up affairs, criminal entanglements, and a governor's second family. Cary was known to have so much power that only a real newbie would dare make a comment about their somewhat unorthodox living arrangements.

"Pardon him, Cary," his client said, trying to mollify him.

Two years ago, before Lucas and Francesca were a permanent part of his life, he would have made the young man sweat. He would have spent the rest of the evening plotting to end his career.

But his life was different now. He cleared his throat and said, "We'll reconvene after the holiday," before ending the meeting.

He might not even destroy the kid's life after the holidays if he hadn't already been fired. He was happy, but he couldn't be seen as having grown soft. From the happy, screeching now coming from their bedroom, going soft wouldn't be a problem for a long while.

He climbed his stairs slowly, savoring the sound of Lucas and Francesca together. A little less than two years ago, he'd almost lost them. He'd almost pushed them away because he didn't think that he deserved to be happy. He'd thought he wouldn't be able to make them happy.

And now he couldn't imagine feeling whole without them.

When he walked into the bedroom, Lucas was eating Francesca's pussy. She pulled his hair with her fingers, and held him in place with her thighs over his broad shoulders. Her mouth was open in the perfect "o" of a silent scream. His timing was perfect, because her back arched and the muscles in her legs tightened in orgasm just as he made his way over to the bed.

He couldn't resist her breasts, so perfectly presented to him. In reality, he didn't even try.

A shiver shook her body when he took her hard nipple into his mouth.

Lucas looked up to him then, and they made eye contact.

LUCAS HADN'T BELIEVED Francesca when she'd told him that the only way to notify Cary that it was quitting time would be to lure him into the bedroom with the sounds of him making her come. He'd gone along with it anyway because he would make her come anytime she asked.

But, to his surprise, it had worked. Just as Frankie's came all over his face, Cary had walked in the room. And now, Lucas met Cary's gaze while he was sucking Francesca's nipple in his mouth.

Lucas wiped off the short beard that he'd grown because Francesca liked it. He wrapped one hand around her thigh because he wasn't done with her yet. She would need to come at least two more times before dinner.

He rose above her and grabbed the back of Cary's too-long hair. His lover's lips were swollen and too tempting for him to resist. He kissed Cary at the same moment that he lined up his dick at Francesca's entrance. She made a desperate, needy sound as she took him inside of her and watched him and Cary kiss.

"Are you feeling neglected, sweet girl?" Lucas asked.

Francesca nodded and bit her bottom lip, but Lucas went right back to kissing Cary. He knew that one of her favorite things was being pinned down like a butterfly specimen while he and Cary forced her to watch them fuck. The greed for their attention mixed with the pleasure she took in seeing them together was a potent mixture that ramped up her desire even more.

This time, Cary stopped and ran his nose up Francesca's neck. She shifted her legs desperately, like she did when she needed a cock, a hand—something to get her off. He loved that they could bring this supremely confident woman to her knees with inarticulate lust. He loved her, treasured her, needed to feel her next to him, over him, underneath him more than he'd ever needed anything.

And, if it were just the two of them, it would scare him. He might not be able to hold all that need. Might not be willing to allow himself to be that vulnerable. Over the past two years, it seemed like everything outside the home he shared with Francesca and Cary had fallen apart, but they only felt more solid.

He never thought he would have wanted to live with anyone, save Cary. But his life was so full with both of his loves in it. So, he made Francesca suffer with want a little more because that was something she needed.

CARY AND LUCAS were perfect when they were like this together, kissing each other as if the other one was air. Making her watch. It was one of their favorite things. Another favorite thing was when she begged, which she was close to doing. She knew that they weren't ignoring her, that she was central to this, that they were making her want it more by pretending that it was just the two of them.

Just as she was about to break, Lucas got rid of the last of Cary's clothes and turned to her. He dipped his head and kissed her mouth as Cary took her nipple into his mouth. She tasted the remains of Cary's tea on Lucas' lips as the latter kissed his way down her belly and spread her legs open with his hands. As Lucas fucked her mouth and pulled her arms over her head, Cary kissed around her pussy, taking his time reaching her clit. His stubble chafed her thighs where Lucas' stubble had already chafed her thighs. Her cunt still felt empty. She ached for Cary's cock, his fingers, or even him wielding something from their toy drawer.

They were so slow with her. She loved it and hated it in equal parts.

She was so glad that Cary and Lucas had been at that restaurant the night that soon-to-be-former Congressman Ted had dumped her. She hadn't realized how lonely she'd been until she'd been with Cary and Lucas for six months. One Saturday, she'd realized that she didn't have to wonder hoe to fill her days. It wasn't just that they would fuck her whenever she demanded it. Cary was always there with a story that Lucas would poke holes in with his well-timed laughs and grunts. Lucas was always there to wrap her in his meaty arms. Someone was always kissing the back of her neck, filling her glass of wine, rubbing her feet while she dashed off e-mails late at night in front of the TV.

A couple of her friends had wondered whether there was jealousy between the three of them—and she could honestly say there was none. The fact that there was three of them didn't make it any less—they were more because of each other.

And she always felt like more when they were fucking, when they worked together to make her writhe and scream with desire. When they showed her how much they loved her with their bodies, with how they fucked each other.

When Lucas let her breathe, she said, "Fuck me."

"Is that what you want for Christmas?" It was a joke—

there was an elaborately wrapped pile of gifts under their tree for the next day. Though she was sure there would be sex toys included among the gifts, that was not what they were talking about here. "No. I want it now."

"What will you give us, love?" Lucas asked between kissed on her neck and collarbone.

The way he was kissing her now, and the way Cary was eating her like she was the best thing he ever tasted had her saying, "Everything."

But then Cary stopped and rose over both of them. His lean, carved body made him look like a god. She certainly worshiped him. "We want more than everything, Francesca."

"Huh?" Francesca struggled to pull her arms out of Lucas' grip.

Cary kissed the other side of her neck as he hooked her thigh around his hip and notched his cock at her entrance. But he didn't work his way his way inside her. "We don't just want everything. We want forever."

"Do we have that from you, love?" Those words from Lucas brought on the realization that Cary and Lucas had planned this. She might have talked Lucas into starting their Christmas celebration early, but this was part of Cary and Lucas' plan all along.

They lived together, and more and more often she was consulting with their clients. People around town had accepted that the three of them were together without too many sideways glances. But they had slipped into this, slowly over time. She'd never asked the increasingly urgent question on her mind—was this her forever?"

"I thought you didn't do forever," she said to Cary.

"I didn't think so either," Cary squeezed the back of Lucas' neck. "Not until I had the two of you."

"Do we have to do this now?" Francesca still wasn't being fucked, and her patience was running thin. They could talk about forever when she'd come again.

Cary smirked at her. "I can't make you come until you agree to spend the rest of your life with us. It's all we want for Christmas, and we're not leaving it to chance."

Francesca looked at Lucas wide-eyed, and he shrugged. "Don't look at me for salvation."

"You're both my salvation. Of course, I want to be with you both," Francesca said. "Forever."

Cary finally sank into her, and Lucas tapped her lips with his cock. "Merry Christmas to us."

THE END

ALSO BY ANDIE J. CHRISTOPHER

One Night in South Beach Series

Stroke of Midnight

Dusk Until Dawn

Break of Day

Before Daylight

Night and Day

All Hours

The Nolans

Not the Girl You Marry

Not That Kind of Guy

Hot Under His Collar

Stand-Alone Rom-Coms

Thank You, Next

Unrealistic Expectations

Erotic Romance

All They Want for Christmas

Full Contact

Biker B*tch

ABOUT THE AUTHOR

USA Today Bestselling author Andie J. Christopher writes sharp, witty, sexy contemporary romance about complex people finding happily ever after. Her work has been featured in NPR, *Cosmopolitan*, *The Washington Post*, *Entertainment Weekly*, and *The New York Post*. Prickly heroines are her hallmark, and she is the originator of the Stern Brunch Daddy. Andie lives in the Nation's Capital with a French bulldog, a stockpile of Campari, and way too many books.

To stay up to date on new releases, join her newsletter!

www.ingramcontent.com/pod-product-compliance
Lightning Source LLC
Chambersburg PA
CBHW051224160726

47994CB00002B/744